Troubled By Love

Tara Kennedy

About This Story

Amy's now ex sent Dan to her, instead of himself. Living in a new city and having to go get an abortion and dump her ex was not how Amy imagined this new chapter of her life going.

Dan has been working hard to get his food truck going. Picking up ride shares, bartending, and barely sleeping, has all been to support that goal. Amy is the first person to make him wonder if he should be finding time for things that aren't work.

After a few months of texting they decide to make a go of it. But when her ex shows up, Amy will have to figure out have things really changed?

Copyright

Content Note

Content Note: This book contains on page abortion, and references to parental cancer and death that occur prior to the book.

Chapter 1

Amy He Metcalfe didn't believe in New Year's resolutions. January was no better month than any other to start changing your life. But four months ago, she had decided to focus a little more on her own goals, and when she was offered a job DC, she had said yes.

DC wasn't far from Philadelphia, where she had gone to college. It was a great opportunity, and her boyfriend Ryder traveled so much she'd see him about the same amount anyway.

She had not counted on finding herself pregnant of course.

Ryder: What time is the appointment?

Amy: 10 am

Amy held onto the phone for another second, but there were no more bubbles indicating he was texting back.

Ryder's job as emergency communications strategist kept him on the move. About six weeks ago, a sudden storm had him in town for an extra day, and they had run out of condoms. Their plans to just use hands and mouths had disappeared.

Amy purchased Plan B at the pharmacy the next day. But she had read all the fine print, and knew Plan B didn't work if you were already pregnant by the time you took it.

Amy knew a lot of stats about both contraception and abortion. She was the eldest of seven kids. Amy had bought her first pack of condoms at ten, placing them prominently at her mother's bedside.

Lots of siblings, especially female siblings knew a lot about middle of the night feedings, diaper changes, making lunches, or back to school shopping on an extreme budget. Amy had gotten any desire to raise kids out of her system well before the school sex ed program came to scare her about teen parenthood.

The sex ed program in Nevada suggested abstinence. Teen Amy had known she couldn't convince her mom of abstinence. Her mom never opened the condoms Amy bought her. The pill, in addition to being expensive, had turned out to have a terrible effect on her mom's depression.

Amy had discovered while she herself as an adult had not previously shown signs of depression, she inherited the same reaction to the pill. She and her ob/gyn had gone through a few of them, before her ob/gyn suggested that condoms had no such side effects. Plan B as a backup was probably better for her mental health.

All of this added up to Amy making a dreaded call to Ryder. She explained she was pregnant, she had an appointment to get the medication necessary to end the pregnancy. She didn't like ultimatums, but he could either get his butt back here or they were officially over. He had agreed to everything.

Then a hurricane hit the Caribbean. Amy had learned to hate hurricanes for many reasons - evidence of climate change, destruction wrought, but also because those bastards sent Ryder places without warning. Ryder should be off the schedule, of course, for the next few days.

Her phone rang and there was a knock on the door. Figuring Ryder had made it from the airport early, she threw open the door without looking, only to find an unfamiliar dark-haired, brown-eyed man standing there. "Next door," Amy said. Her neighbor had a lot of friends and often they knocked on her door by accident.

"Amy?" he said.

Amy stopped swinging the door closed. She knew better than to confirm her name to a stranger, but the folks looking for her neighbor Helena never knew her name.

Her phone chirped one more time and then went silent.

"I'm Dan," stranger dude said, "and I think that was Ryder calling to warn you. I made good time."

Amy wanted to slam the door now. It wasn't stranger dude's fault. Dan. Stranger dude's name was Dan. If Ryder had sent a stranger to her door, he wasn't on a plane. Not to here at least.

"Is it the hurricane?" Amy asked. It wasn't a question that would make sense to anyone who didn't know Ryder.

Dan shook his head. "Mudslide in Japan."

"So, Ryder sent you to what - spend the night?" Amy asked. Part of her, a stupid hopeful part, was still crushed that just this freaking once, Ryder hadn't taken himself off the schedule. He could. His other coworkers did. Amy was nothing if not an expert at looking strong when she was crushed inside.

"I think the idea was for us to chat a bit before tomorrow. To make it less awkward." Dan grimaced a bit, as if he realized the awkward train had long ago left the station.

"Darling," Helena said, leaning out of her door, long strawberry blonde hair loose. "As fascinating as this has all been, could you either let him in or kick him out. Any minute now, Mrs. Overgaard is going to email the whole building."

"Thanks, Helena," Amy said flatly.

Helena smiled and shut her door.

Helena was right though. The building was old enough that the soundproofing between apartments was good, but hallway conversations carried. Mrs. Overgaard often sent emails to everyone in the building reminding them of courtesy and decorum. "Come on in, I guess," Amy said.

Probably, Ryder's friend Dan wasn't a serial killer. And if he was, well, Amy didn't have a plan for that. Her plan for Ryder not showing up had been to go to the clinic herself. She'd been assured the pills were fairly painless, and had stocked up on super-strength pads, a bunch of microwave meals, and sports drinks. She had a streaming list of silly, lighthearted comedies, and dark revenge dramas, for her every mood.

She sat dead center on the couch, in her partially unpacked living room. Having to find the Planned Parenthood clinic her first week in DC had not been on her to do list. Nor had asking for a planned sick day before she'd had a chance to accrue any leave. Her boss had been great about it, made sure Amy had enough funds. But Amy had hoped that was it. That was enough awkward and uncomfortable at least for the month, but she should have known. The universe had endless wells of awkward and uncomfortable, and when it decided it was your turn, it was like a mudslide.

DAN REES HAD KNOWN Ryder since they were teenagers. Dan had grown up in DC, and Ryder in Pennsylvania, but their families had both been Unitarian Universalists, and so they had met at a regional family summer camp for UUs. When his mom had gotten too sick to go, they had figured on missing a year. But the Rivette family had picked Dan up and let him stay in their cabin for the week so that Dan could get some fun in.

So, Dan had known Ryder long enough, the bond was deep enough, that when Ryder called and said, "Hey, my girlfriend has a medical procedure tomorrow, and I'm not going to make it. Could you go say hi, I'll clear it with her." - Dan had said okay.

Standing in Amy's living room, looking at her dark hair, yoga pants, and a t-shirt faded from several years of washings, he was rethinking this. Between Ryder and Dan's hectic schedules, he'd barely seen Ryder in person in the last few years. He'd heard about but never met Amy. Amy didn't seem to have any info about him.

Dan was torn between making an excuse to leave and hugging her. The dark circles under her eyes told him sleep had been hard to come by. Working as a rideshare driver to supplement his income while he awaited permit approval on his food truck, he knew what someone who'd been running themselves ragged looked like. So yeah, he was going to try to stay. At least long enough to convince her to let him drive her tomorrow.

She had plopped in the middle of the couch. Looking around the living room, he found a lone chair next to a small table and flipped it around to sit facing her.

"So, Ryder was calling you to tell you, but he and I go way back. I realize that doesn't fix the stranger to you part, but he did want to make sure you had someone with you tomorrow."

Dan had put two and two together and was pretty clear what type of medical appointment a woman would want her boyfriend taking her to. Ryder had sounded very apologetic on the phone, but Dan was sure that was very little comfort to Amy. Ryder and the Rivette family had been rocks for him and his dad. Dan was happy to return the favor, but this was not quite the same. However, he was sure at least not having to worry about transportation to the appointment was something he could help out with.

Amy picked up her phone and tossed it back down on the couch. "He's boarded the plane, but yeah, he says you'll do everything he would have done. Let's assume he didn't think that sentence all the way through."

Yeesh. Yeah. "Well, I make great soup, so if you tell me your favorite, I can bring some when I pick you up tomorrow."

"You don't have to pick me up just because Ryder told you you should," Amy said. "I'll be fine."

"I know," Dan said. "But please let me."

"I can call a cab or whatever."

"I technically am a cab or whatever, emphasis on the whatever," Dan said. "So think of it as saving a step."

"Okay."

They exchanged numbers, confirmed the time she wanted to leave, and Dan knew he should go. She may need to cry, scream, or do any other number of things it would be odd to do in front of a stranger.

"Oh, soup," he said.

"I bought a bunch of microwave thingies," Amy said, her hand waving in the direction of the fridge.

"I've got lentil, squash, and curried cauliflower in my freezer,." Dan said.

"Fine."

Dan nodded. "Do you have everything you need to get some sleep?"

"I'll be fine."

Dan nodded again and stood. "Okay, I'll see you tomorrow."

He paused in the hallway until he heard the lock click behind him, taking the stairs down a floor and out to his car. Amy's appointment tomorrow was late enough he'd hopefully be able to park right in front of the building.

He texted Ryder that he'd talked to Amy. It was a Wednesday night, so Xavier was unlikely to need him at the bar. He did text Xavier that he might not be available this weekend, sick friend. Dan wasn't on the schedule this week, but the others knew he would often pick up shifts if they needed backup.

He drove to the grocery store where he picked up a bunch of ingredients. He'd told Amy the truth, he had tons of soup in his freezer. But sometimes chicken ginger soup and maybe a baked potato soup were what you needed. Making soup tonight would give him time to think about what it meant that somehow his longtime friend Ryder's idea of a favor had turned into please take my girlfriend to the clinic to get an abortion.

AMY LOOKED AT THE PHONE. Ryder's plane ride to Japan would take hours. They should have this conversation in person. Of course, his not being here was why they needed to have the conversation.

Amy: Stay safe in Japan. I told you if you couldn't take yourself off the schedule for me this one time, that was it. I meant it. Sending your friend doesn't count. So, we're done now.

Her finger hovered over the send button. Amy expected to feel something but she felt empty. Sometimes being the oldest sibling meant getting used to everyone else getting what they wanted first. Amy had hoped getting away, to college, to the East Coast, would help. Ryder was part of the pattern she needed to leave behind. She pressed send.

Chapter 2

The day of the procedure felt almost anticlimactic. Amy was tempted to toss salt over her shoulder and spit twice for even thinking of such a thing. Dan had shown up as promised, he hadn't tried to be chatty or weird. He had quickly corrected the nurse that he was just a friend, but politely not in a way that made it seem like he was disavowing Amy. She'd been able to get both medications in a single visit and now they were headed back to her place.

Dan found parking and made her wait while he popped the trunk to grab a soft cooler bag, and then insisted on helping her out of the car.

"I can walk," Amy said. But she took his arm anyway. She'd known Dan less than twenty-four hours, but she knew he was going to stand there with his arm out until she took it.

Ms. Overgaard peeked out of her door at them. Amy pretended she couldn't see her. She was not up to Ms. Overgaard's insistent concern.

She opened the door to her apartment and moved straight for the couch. They had warned her this was going to feel like a pretty major period, and already she could feel that leaden feeling in her uterus like it was deciding exactly how much crud to expel. She had stashed a few bottles of sports drink right on the side table that morning and the laptop was right on the couch, with her shows ready to queue up.

Dan had gone over to her fridge. "I brought you three different kinds of soup. Do you want me to heat one up before I go?"

Amy didn't feel hungry. She'd need food for sure later, but right now she just wanted to zone out in front of a show. "I'm good. Thanks for the ride. You definitely went above and beyond."

"I'll go, but I'll check in with you by text tomorrow. If you need something, let me know. And if you don't answer, I'll be forced to get creative, so answer, even if it's to tell me to go away."

"Got it." Amy nodded.

He patted her shoulder and then left. She got up and locked the door, shuffling back to the couch.

She had a rom-com started when the phone chirped. Picking it up, she sighed when she saw it was Ryder. She had known that texting still meant they were going to have a conversation.

"Hi," she said.

"How are you doing, babe? I'm still screwed up from the time change, but you had the appointment right, did everything go okay?"

"Don't call me babe," Amy said. She had never liked it, and he knew that.

"Oh, come one Ame, I'm really sorry I couldn't be there, but who could have predicted two disasters would hit this week?"

"Thousands of climatologists?" Amy said. "But that isn't the point. I told you this was it. I wasn't putting my life to the side every time it was convenient for you."

"Amy, I'm sorry, and I know this is an emotional day for you, so maybe we just table this discussion for later."

Amy didn't feel emotional, she felt tired. There were so many things she liked about Ryder, the long- distance stuff had never seemed like a hardship. Sure, he could rarely make it back for things like friend's weddings. They had never been able to plan a vacation together longer than two days. There were lots of couples that dealt with distance, and far more danger than Ryder was generally in, so she had been fine with it.

But she had accepted a new job and planned a move and barely been able to speak to him about it, because he'd been somewhere with limited service. He had come back to help her celebrate and theoretically help her pack, but instead he'd invited twelve other people to their celebration dinner. They'd gotten home late, engaged in some personal celebration. And then the storm had delayed his departure, leading to an extra night when they were out of condoms.

Amy was tired of always having to be the one who was patient and understanding, neither of these were particular strengths of hers. She was tired of being talked out of what she wanted. Tired of not having any sort of priority in Ryder's life.

"Amy?" Ryder said.

That was the other thing, Amy had grown so used to not being able to talk to Ryder when she needed to, that she could have whole conversations with him in her head. Lately these conversations were all arguments.

"I'm tired of only being able to argue with you in my head. I'm not emotional, Ryder. Or not more so than usual. I told you if you couldn't be here for my abortion, then I was out. Either you didn't believe me or you think there was some sort of footnote to that."

"Babe," Ryder said.

Amy hung up on him. She should cry or something, right? Because she had ended a relationship with someone she loved and had an abortion. But her eyes felt dry.

She just felt hollow. She tried to think about how she had planned to get to know DC so well, so she could show it off to Ryder the next time he was stateside. Not today, of course, even in her wildest dreams, she had only imagined Ryder would be here for a day or two.

It was a good thing Amy didn't want kids, because yeah, she might have inherited her taste in men from her mom after all.

Chapter 3

Dan: Hey, this is Dan, checking in. Did you eat something?

Amy: I have you saved in my phone, Dan. And yes, I did.

DAN: I WAS TESTING out a batch of pesto soup. Do you want me to bring some over?

Amy: I still have plenty of food. So, I'm okay thanks. But the chicken ginger soup was really yummy. Thanks for giving me some.

Dan: Anything else you need? I'm driving around today, so easy for me to stop by you.

Amy: I'm good but thanks.

DAN: ANYTHING YOU NEED?

Amy: I'm feeling much better today. Ready to get back to the normal routine.

Dan: Okay. Would you tell me if it was otherwise?

Amy: I might. But I really am doing well. Thanks for checking. Also, you should know, I broke up with Ryder.

Dan: I'm sorry to hear that. Since my number's saved remember I can help out if needed. I'm sure being in a new city is tough.

Amy: I appreciate it.

Chapter 4

One Month Later

"Come on, it'll be fun," Lillian said, her brown eyes glinting, or maybe it was a reflection from the streetlights.

"This is your brother's bar?" Amy asked. She and Lillian had met at a knitting meetup two weeks ago when Amy had decided to try to make some non-work friends. Lillian was one of those people who glommed onto folks and wouldn't let go. For some reason Amy found this amusing rather than irritating. She hadn't quite figured out why.

"No," Lillian said. "At my brother's bar, the hot bartender is my brother, and also literally everyone who works there knows me and reports everything I do to him. As if I'm the one who needs looking after. Pfft. No, this is my brother's friend's bar."

"And your brother's friend doesn't report back to your brother?"

Lillian's smile became knowing. "Not so far."

Amy wondered if that meant she was really signing up to watch Lillian flirt tonight. That sounded better than go to a bar to meet guys plural. Definitely better than ducking calls from Ryder. He'd accepted the breakup. Despite being able to invite eight other people to dinner at a moment's notice, he seemed to like talking to her. She liked talking to him, but decided she needed to get out and do things with people that were not her ex.

Amy tried a bunch of things, book club, knitting, protests, kayaking. The knitting, well, she wasn't going to chuck it all and open an Etsy shop anytime soon. But she had made a cowl. And liked it enough to try something else.

And met Lillian. Who she liked enough to hang out with outside of knitting.

"Okay," Amy said.

"Yay. Should we call a car?" Lillian asked.

"Can't we metro?" Amy asked.

"I guess," Lillian said in an exaggerated tone of resign.

The metro train got them to the stop quickly, and Lillian led them to the correct exit and across street lit city streets. She clearly took this route a lot. They crossed from a residential block full of rowhouses, to a small stretch of more commercial looking buildings with flat roofs.

There were bars over the high windows, but the signage looked clean and modern. Walking inside, the noise level was medium. A long L-shaped bar bisected the space, with bar stools, and a skinnier bar along the wall. Lillian found a space in the people seated at the bar and leaned through, smiling at a guy with dark wavy hair.

She looked behind her and gestured to Amy.

"Amy, this is Xavier. Tell him what you want."

"Hi, Amy," Xavier said.

Amy didn't see anyone holding menus, so went for an old standby, "Sea breeze please."

Xavier nodded.

"Xavier," Lillian said, "where are we going to sit?"

Amy scanned the room. It looked like there might be an empty stool across the room, but quite a few people were standing, so they might need to hover a bit.

Xavier shrugged, leaning down to grab a bottle, clearly not concerned with the answer.

Amy and Lillian chatted with their drinks, eventually managing to swoop in and grab two chairs. "So, what about you?" Lillian asked. "Any hotness for you or should I keep an eye out for someone?"

"Nah, I got out of a relationship right after I moved here, so not ready for all that yet."

"Oh, that sucks." Lillian sipped her drink. "How long was the relationship?"

"Almost three years. Although if you add up the amount of time we actually spent together, it's less."

"Oh wow," Lillian said. "It's definitely time for you to try on someone new. It doesn't have to be like a whole relationship. What about Mateo?"

Lillian pointed to the other guy, working the bar. He had dark straight hair and Amy noticed he regularly checked on the woman carrying glasses and other things back and forth from the backroom. Sure, he could just be a conscientious employee checking in on his co-worker, but Amy had a vibe there was a little more to it. Also, Mateo was attractive, but Amy felt only intellectual interest. Much like looking at a picture of a celebrity. She could see that the parts came together attractively, but it was meaningless to her.

She didn't usually fall for the hotness, the way some of her friends did. She had known Ryder all through college and hadn't been remotely interested in him until they ended up on the same trivia team at an alumni happy hour, and then all of sudden wham. Maybe she should find a trivia team.

"Okay, I'll stop pressuring you," Lillian said.

"No it's fine, I tend not to go for visuals so much," Amy said.

"Gotcha. Well, and just because I feel like life is inherently better with orgasms, doesn't mean everyone has to agree with me." Lillian's smile brightened.

Xavier paused, "You two doing okay here?"

"Just talking about orgasms," Lillian said.

Xavier gave a thumbs up and continued on.

"Just so I'm clear," Amy said, "are we trying to embarrass him or what?"

"He's unembarassable as far as I can tell." Lillian sipped her drink.

"So, is this like the guards at the palace in London?" Amy asked. "You're trying to see if you can get a reaction."

"No," Lillian said, "mostly I'm just reminding him, that I am a person with needs, wants, and desires."

Two drinks later, Amy switched to water. She enjoyed chatting with Lillian, but also wanted to be functional tomorrow, even if all she had to look forward to was a day of laundry. Lillian showed no signs of slowing, and Amy didn't want to leave her alone at the bar. The clientele had shifted in the bar, from casual office clothes to more folks in jeans, black, and shirts with restaurant logos.

"Your brother is on his way," Xavier said.

"And that's my cue." Lillian tossed money on the bar.

Amy grabbed cash and tossed some out. "Do you want to split a car?"

They were just past the last metro train time, especially since Lillian and Amy would both need to switch trains.

Lillian leaned all the way across the bar, beckoning to Xavier. She whispered in his ear. Amy watched and yeah, Xavier's poker face was very good. He nodded and then Lillian smiled and grabbed Amy's arm, walking outside.

Amy requested a car through the app. "Did you want to split the ride home? And you want to tell me why we're leaving here like we're underage?"

"I'm not going straight home," Lillian said, "but I'll wait with you until your car comes. Safety and solidarity."

"Ah," Amy said. While that wasn't a direct answer to her second question, Amy had a pretty good idea. Her phone pinged three times in succession.

A car pulled up and the window down. "Amy?" the driver asked.

Amy checked the driver info, a shiver skimming the back of her neck. Daniel, Honda Civic, it said. Oh. "Hi, Dan," she said. Amy wasn't ready to process what it meant to run into Dan. She popped open the door and turned to Lillian. "You want us to give you a ride where you're going?"

Lillian smiled and pointed to a rowhouse across the street. "I am going right there."

"Okay, see you next week." Amy hugged Lillian and slid into the car.

Amy thought perhaps her ability to make small talk had been obliterated by the twin things of alcohol and tired. Sitting in the car, in the back felt weird. Talking felt weird. Not talking felt weird.

His texts had petered off after a few days, and she'd kept wanting to restart the conversation. Like, hey, want to hang out sometime when I don't need an abortion. She had hoped to run into him. Now here he was, and she couldn't figure out what to say.

DAN HAD PICKED UP PASSENGERS he knew before in his car. Having grown up in the area, having gone to school here, he knew quite a few people here. Some of them were exactly the folks that used rideshare apps to get home after dinner out, or home from Sunday brunch. There were generally two kinds of reactions.

They either pretended like they didn't know him and got very busy either chatting with whoever else was in the car with them or on their phones. Or they acted so incredibly happy and surprised to see him and then asked him if he just did this or had another job or maybe seventeen secret kids. Sometimes he explained that no, he was building up extra money for his food truck, but a lot of times he didn't. If they didn't find him worth talking to as a rideshare driver, then he didn't think food truck was going to impress them. After all, working as a taxi or rideshare driver was as valid as any other job.

Amy looked kind of amazing tonight. Her hair looked wavier than he remembered, she was wearing makeup, and had on slim cut pants with a flowy top. She still looked like herself of course, but it was great to see her looking a little tired because it was one in the morning, not because she'd just had an emotional and physically exhausting day. He wanted to talk to her, find out how she was doing. He didn't know how to start that conversation. He glanced in the rear view mirror and caught her yawning.

"So, I have a question?" Amy asked.

He glanced in the mirror again. She had leaned forward. The air molecules along his shoulder buzzed in alert. "Yes?" he asked.

"The chicken ginger soup was amazing. I thanked you for that right?"

"You did." Once she had texted him that she was ready to go back to normal, he hadn't wanted to keep bugging her. It was nice to see she was indeed doing okay.

"Is soup making like knitting for you or is it like your job?" Amy asked. "Sorry, I'm tired, that made more sense in my head."

Dan smiled. "I think I got it. Right now, it's a side gig. I am working on getting a food truck. Well, I have the truck. I rent kitchen space and sell at some farmers markets for now. We almost have everything finalized to get the truck started too. I had hoped for winter, but the food inspector asked for some changes to the truck. And sorry, that was a long answer." Most of his friends had reached the tell me when there is something new stage of his discussions with everything. Dan never grew tired of talking about his dreams and was happy to have a new audience.

"I asked. So cool. You'll tell me when the truck is up and running, so I can come find you right?"

"Yes. Trust me everyone I know will know." Dan would have included her anyway, but was glad to have a reason to specifically tell her.

"Good."

Dan made the last turn, finding the spot right in front of her building again. He was sort of sad to be ending the ride. Hopefully he could pick up one more ride for the night. Different bars in DC had different closing times based on a combination of licensing and neighborhood agreements. Places like Xavier's, and a few of the clubs, hadn't quite closed for the night.

"Here we are," he said. Of course, she knew where she lived. He ended the ride in the app to cover his frustration.

"It was great to see you, Dan. Text me about the soup." She slid out the door, waved on the sidewalk and went upstairs. Her apartment was on the back side of the building, so he could sit here and watch, but he wouldn't be able to see her light go on. So, he pulled away, awaiting another ride request.

Chapter 5

Amy: Can I ask you a question?

Dan: Other than that one? Sure.

Amy: ...

Dan: Sorry, childhood reflex.

Amy: Well, now I have two questions.

Dan: Go for it.

Amy: The original question was is it weird to drive folks you know? Like, I was relieved to see it was you. But maybe it's weird.

Dan: It's not weird. Unless the person I pick up makes it weird. But you didn't.

Amy: Good. Okay, childhood reflex? Do you have siblings?

Dan: No, just cousins, but they definitely kept me on guard. Still do.

Amy: Ah.

Dan: Do you have siblings? Assuming I'm allowed to ask questions.

Amy: Of course you are. And I have six siblings at last count.

Dan: Wow. That's a lot.

Amy: Tell me about it.

Dan: Your parents must really like kids.

Amy: My mom really likes sex. Sorry. TMI. I think my mom likes the idea of kids more than the reality. Everyone's alive and well cared for. Her current boyfriend is great. Okay, that was definitely TMI. How's the truck?

Dan: One last permit and then we're in business.

Amy: Exciting. Do food trucks do like a grand opening or something?

Dan: Yeah. I will let you know.

Amy: Good.

DAN: WHAT ARE YOU DOING for lunch tomorrow? Actually, you know what? I realized I don't know where your office is? This is Dan by the way.

Amy: You're still saved in my phone, Dan. This is Amy by the way. My office is by Farragut North.

Dan: Ah, well, I'm going to aim for being at Franklin Square tomorrow, so close by. One of the other vendors is letting me take their spot.

Amy: Well, I can take a long lunch, especially if delicious soup will be available. What are the debut flavors going to be?

Dan: Oh, I see, looking for insider information here.

Amy: Yep, I'm using you for soup previews.

Dan: My soup previews are fantastic.

Amy: Got a little weird there.

Dan: I don't have to tell you.

Amy: Okay, I apologize. I am awaiting this news with bated breath. How do you even bate breath? Never mind, I am sure my breath has been bated.

Dan: Chicken ginger, cauliflower, and a tomato white bean soup.

Amy: Oh my gosh. They all sound great.

Dan: Hopefully the rest of the lunch crowd agrees.

Amy: I'm sure they will. It's on my calendar. Congrats!

Chapter 6

"Sadami, ready come with me to grab lunch?" Amy leaned against the door frame of his office.

"Two minutes?" he held up two fingers.

"Sure." Amy sat in his guest chair and tried not to fidget.

Sadami kept typing but glanced over at her. "Okay, clearly we need to go visit your guy now." He knocked on the office wall. "Faith, we're going to see Amy He's soup guy."

"I'm ready," Faith said appearing in the doorway, purse on her shoulder.

"Are you guys going to be embarrassing?" Amy asked. She knew once you asked, the chances were already about seventy-five percent.

"We just like to make sure everything is alright with our newest co-worker," Faith said.

Amy rolled her eyes. She grabbed her phone.

Amy: Hey, Dan. Bringing some coworkers who I apologize in advance for, but they brought money.

Dan maybe wouldn't be able to check his phone during what she hoped was turning out to be a super successful lunch rush, but hoped when he checked later, he'd forgive her. Hopefully. Dan was pretty easygoing.

"What's the food truck called?" Faith asked.

The light changed, and they crossed the street onto Franklin Square. The food trucks lined up along one side of the park. In addition to the statue of some naval looking dude, there were grassy areas, trees, benches and pathways. All in one park with enough space for about eight food trucks along one side, and a bunch of metro buses along another.

The day was crisp but sunny. The lines in front of each truck were pretty long. The truck on the end had a line that wrapped around the corner and around a tree. Amy pulled up the text chain with Dan, trying to remember what he had called the truck. It had been something odd. Wow, they had a lot of texts. "Bull Lion," Amy said. "Oh my god I just got that."

"Huh?" Faith said.

"Bull Lion, you put it together and you have-"

"Bullion," Sadami said. "It's something alright. Well, the line is long. You can share this gem with lots of other people."

"I like it," Faith said.

"You like it now that it's been explained to you,. Sadami said. Sadami was their communications strategist. "Most people won't get it."

"So someone will tell them," Faith said. "Most people don't know what or who a Popeye is either. They still eat there."

"Fine. But Popeye's is an old institution."

"No work talk," Amy said. They could and did have these debates for hours. Amy still had stress flashbacks from the initiative naming discussion.

"So," Faith said, "Does that mean it's time for talk about your personal life?"

"You mean my knitting?" Amy said.

"I do not mean your knitting," Faith said. "How do you know soup guy?"

"He's a friend of a friend," Amy said. Explaining Dan was a friend of her ex sounded weird. She had never met Dan while she was dating Ryder. Ryder had introduced her to lots of people, made friends everywhere, but Dan had only come up in passing.

The running joke among Ryder's coworkers was that Ryder would always cover any day the others needed off, because he never blocked himself off. Amy hadn't been counting on no natural disasters hitting during a three day period during disaster season, she had been counting on Ryder for once taking himself out of the rotation. And he wouldn't. So, by the time Dan knocked on her door, she had known things with Ryder were over, because she shouldn't have needed an ultimatum to get him to show up.

So in Amy's head she met Dan because of Ryder, but he wasn't part of her time with Ryder.

"So you knew him when you were in Philly?" Sadami asked,

"No," Amy said, "I met him here. He lives here. He's from here."

"Oh cool," Faith said. "I should find out what school he went to. Gotta support the local boys."

"You got in line before you knew he was local," Sadami said.

"Yes, but now I'm more excited."

Sadami rolled his eyes. Amy got them talking about a sitcom. The line moved at a good pace, and perhaps because of the weather or the excitement of something new, no one in the line seemed or upset that they were spending so long in line. This section of the city had a lot of lobby firms and consultants, part of the reason her non-profit had offices here, to be near other power brokers. She had seen people get very mad at the time the fast casual place took to make their meal, or if a fast food place was only willing to make four substitutions to the meal.

They were now close enough that she could see Dan poking his head in and out of the window, chatting with folks, and calling out orders for pick up.

One woman at the front of the line seemed to be involved in an excessive amount of hair flipping, surely soup ordering did not call for hair flipping.

Dan's expression remained friendly but polite.

They finally made it to the front.

Faith was first. "Hey, I need a small tomato white bean and to know what school you went to, since I understand you're local."

"I am." He leaned forward, propping his elbows on the counter, "should I answer before or after I tell you about the three stars two bars discount?"

"Oh, definitely let's do the discount, then share details. Just in case there are rivalries involved."

"Although I find, the transplant vs. local rivalry seems to outpace everything. Not that I don't love all my customers, even the new arrivals." He winked in Amy's direction.

Amy felt that wink though she did her best to keep her expression neutral. These were her co-workers, this was his workplace, and the only thing she expected to leave this truck with was soup. Not tingles, not additional warmth, not a sudden interest in knowing if Dan had a special someone in his life.

"So, is there a friends discount?" Amy asked wanting to snatch back the words. It had sounded flirty in her head, instead now it seemed greedy.

Dan smiled and winked at her again. "There's actually an opening day discount, but ssh, don't tell," he said softly. Looking over at the sign she saw the chalkboard said, grand opening discount. Oh, maybe that was why people had been so patient in line.

She ordered a small of each , and moved to the side so Sadami could make his order. Faith tugged her back on the grass, so the line could keep moving. "You have so got it bad," she said quietly."

Sadami stepped over to them so Amy decided pretending she hadn't heard Faith was the safest choice. They could talk later. Not here. Not where Dan could hear. Not while she was still figuring out what it meant that she might like Dan.

DAN SHOULD BE TIRED, would be the second he sat down anywhere. Right now, the numbers looked good for the first day, and he had seen lots of people who promised to come back.

"Thanks, Mateo." Dan handed him his share of the tip jar. Mateo also worked at Xavier's. Mateo had daytime hours available and had been willing to take the food certification course with Dan.

"So, how many of the customers today were your friends and family?" Mateo asked.

"Only a few of my cousins showed up today. A few were people I knew from high school, or church, or from work." Dan's dad lived in Delaware now and was driving down tomorrow. The cousins had promised to text him pictures.

"So, half."

"Not half." Dan chuckled. "But yeah. Tomorrow we're on our own, but the Latvian truck, the owner's mom is in the hospital, so they are cool with me taking their lottery spots for this week. Next week we might have to bounce around more." DC had more than enough hungry office workers to go around. The challenge was there was a booming food truck community and everyone liked to rotate through prime hot spots like this. The licensing board kept tweaking the rules to try and create more equitable access.

Right now, a number of spots were assigned by lottery. Next month he'd be able to submit Bull Lion on its own. For the rest of the month, he was relying on people being willing to give up their slot or finding a place where he was allowed to park for a few hours that wasn't part of the lottery. Dan had been working on getting to know fellow food truck owners, building up relationships with festivals and farmer's markets. And while he hoped the Latvian truck owner's mom was okay, it had worked out nicely for him and so far, none of the other owners seemed to mind.

"Okay," Mateo said, "same time, or you want me to meet you at the kitchen earlier?"

"Same time is good. Thanks, man."

Mateo gave him a back- slapping hug and was out of there.

Dan got the truck locked up for the night, and headed home with a sandwich one of the other food truck vendors had given him in exchange for some soup.

Seated on his bed, he flipped on the TV and tried to massage his feet. Bartending he had gotten used to standing for long hours. Getting up early to make soup in a health inspector certified kitchen, followed by a long lunch window, and a dinner window, meant longer hours on his feet than the typical bar shift.

He'd get used to it. The first few weeks working the rideshare had been tough too, until he found the right seat setting so his butt didn't fall asleep and his thighs didn't cramp up.

His phone pinged.

Amy: I loved all the soups but the chicken ginger is still my favorite.

Dan: So noted.

He smiled.

Amy: Now that you are a successful soup mogul, are you giving up the rideshare life?

Dan: Not yet. But if you need a ride somewhere, you can always ask me.

Amy: Oh, thanks, but no I was more asking if maybe this meant you'd get more free time. Or I guess different free time.

Dan: Probably different free time.

Dan did miss free time.

Dan: Although we'll see what next month's parking lottery brings.

Amy: Oh my gosh, I have so many questions.

Dan: Shoot.

He was bone tired, the adrenaline from the first day having drained away. Texting with Amy was far more interesting than the movie he had queued up. It was nice talking with someone who wasn't bored with all his plans. But also, it was nice talking to Amy. She was Ryder's ex, so probably into flashier guys than him. But this was just texting.

Amy: Actually, no, you had a long day and I have google. But I realized I don't know something important.

Dan: Okay.

Dan wondered what it was. It could be anything, from his favorite sports team to his favorite sex position.

Amy: What is it you do for fun?

Dan smiled.

Dan: Remind me what fun is again? I'm too tired to google.

Amy: Ah, and now I see what you and Ryder have in common.

Yeah, Dan was pretty sure that was not a compliment even if it was somewhat accurate. Ryder was always on the go. If Ryder said he could be somewhere, there was about a fifty percent chance he would make it. But when he was there, his attention to detail his focus, it was amazing. Dan's dad always asked after that nice young Ryder.

So what did Dan do for fun? Drinking coffee probably wasn't enough of a thing.

Dan: I like museums.

He watched anxiously for the reply bubbles. He didn't usually tell people about that. He wasn't embarrassed or anything, but museums were a thing he could do alone, quietly. Whenever he was stuck on a recipe, a walk through the Sculpture Garden or an art exhibit would give him perspective. Or it distracted him long enough that he solved it. Either way, it was his version of a beach vacation, and much more suitable to the budget of a small business owner since most of the museums in DC were free.

Amy: Cool. Do you have a favorite museum? I keep meaning to go to some, but I have no idea where to start.

Dan: No wrong answers. They are all different. What was your favorite one in Philly?

Amy: The Franklin Institute.

Dan had gone there with his dad one day as a kid. His mom had been visiting some specialists in Philadelphia. The science museum was highly interactive, so a great distraction.

Dan: Natural History might work for you. It's not science focused in the same way, but has some more interactive type stuff than some of the others."

Amy: Cool. I'll take a look. Okay, I'll let you sleep.

"Good night," he texted. Sleep was the right choice for now. This multi-hyphenate life was a lot. He had been so close to having everything lined up when the pandemic hit and tanked his savings, and threw off the timing for opening a new food truck when no one knew where the workers were going to be. But it meant he was still picking up ride share shifts, still working bar shifts, and still making the rounds of the farmers markets, and launching a food truck. So the sleep schedule was important. But texting Amy made him smile, so there was that.

Chapter 7

Amy: Hey, got trapped in the meeting from hell, but I hope you had a great day too.

Dan: We did. Did you get lunch?

Amy: I did. No worries there.

AMY: WHAT MAGIC IS in the spinach soup?

Dan: A hearty base broth, chickpeas, spinach, and then of course topped with roasted chickpeas and yogurt.

Amy: So there's not like sugar, chocolate, or, I dunno, something addictive in there? Something that would explain why it sounds and looks like a healthy smoothie and yet tastes delicious enough that I want more.

Dan: No secret ingredients. And I'm not just saying that because the food inspector requires me to disclose.

Amy: Those darn food inspectors.

Dan: Ah, well. Here's hoping enough people like soup smoothies.

AMY: I DON'T KNOW IF answering this violates superstition, but what happens if you kill a soup accidentally in the morning.

Dan: Kill it like ruin it?

Amy: Yeah

Dan: Vegetable medley.

Amy: ???

Dan: Vegetable medley is quick, easy, and can be put together in infinite combinations. No one will tell you, no no, real vegetable medley soup must have peas. So, you can throw it together from whatever ingredients, the cooking time is relatively short, and you can add spices to make up for mediocre vegetables.

Amy: There are mediocre vegetables?

Dan: Oh yeah.

Amy: Huh, I usually do not think of vegetables with that much nuance.

Dan: Job hazard. You probably have some too.

Amy: Well, non-profit job hazards make you that person at the cocktail party who wants to talk about poverty initiatives. So, more like a need to have some good TV to talk about because the people who want to talk poverty initiatives at bars are never the fun ones.

Dan: You probably have hobbies too.

Amy: Reading. And I started knitting. That's how I met that girl I was with the night you picked me up.

Dan: Lillian.

Amy: You know Lillian? Do you know everyone?

Dan: Not hardly. But Mateo who works with me on the food truck and I both have worked at that bar. So I have met Lillian.

Amy: Huh. She didn't say anything. Wow, the world really is small.

Amy: She says she thought I knew. And, well, yeah. I am also supposed to say hi. She's been trying to convince her boss to let her take a long lunch break to visit the truck but no luck yet. Apparently Xavier says no soup in the bar.

Dan: Bar's license doesn't allow for food.

Amy: Well, maybe I'll pick up some extra for her. What's on the menu for tomorrow?

Dan: Using me for my inside information again, I see.

Amy: Oh dear, you've caught on to my secret plan.

Amy: Are you really not going to tell me?

Amy: I was kidding btw. You don't have to tell me.

Dan: I am so sorry. I fell asleep. Should not have laid down to text.

Chapter 8

Amy: I feel very soupless.

The lottery for the key spots in DC had not gone in Dan's favor this month. So far, no one with a lottery spot had a sick relative. At least not that he knew of. There were more farmers markets starting up as the weather warmed, so he had some more things opening up.

But Dan could definitely do something for a favored customer.

Dan: I can bring you some soup.

Amy: I know, but I liked walking over for lunch. Also, which farmers market will you be at this weekend? No wait, new question. Do you have to farmers market both Saturday and Sunday? When do you get a day off?

That was the million- dollar question. Well, it probably wasn't worth quite that much, if his bank account was anything to go by.

Dan: Right now, I've got quite a few evenings and afternoons off.

A lot of the parking spaces, especially the ones not included in the lottery, changed over to no parking to allow for more traffic during rush hour. So, instead of trying to find somewhere there might be dinner folks, they had been packing up and going to get ready for the next day. The evenings were light enough for him to justify skipping either taking a shift at the bar or trying to catch pick up some rides. At least until they got to Thursday through Sunday. Then if Xavier didn't have a bar shift for him, he'd grab what rides he could.

Launching a new business meant cash outlays, and the vagaries of the lottery system meant more uncertainty. Of course, it worked both ways, if DC didn't have a lottery system for the more coveted spots, he'd have to have waited essentially for one of the regulars to quit or retire to make a space for him. Or take his chances in one of the suburbs, where he'd have to pass totally different food and health inspection rules.

After a year, he was willing to reevaluate and see if he'd be better off aiming for the lower competition suburbs, but he wanted to get through a year. That's why he was still in this tiny basement apartment that was probably technically illegal and therefore a steal on rent.

Amy: Which ones, give me a time? And I get that sometimes it's not predictable.

Dan: Tuesday.

Tuesday was slow for both bar shifts and rideshare. He usually came home after grocery shopping and watched a movie or two.

Amy: Okay, so next Tuesday can I get you to come hang at a museum with me. We can grab food after, my treat.

Dan: You don't have to.

Amy: You've been feeding me, it's only fair.

Dan: You paid for that food.

Amy: Don't care. Still my turn.

Dan: Okay, Tuesday.

He usually traded lunch with fellow food truck owners. It would be refreshing to eat some food actually sitting down somewhere. Seeing Amy would also be great. They were just friends, of course. Nothing more. But he could make time for friends.

Chapter 9

Amy checked the time on the corner of her computer display again. She checked her phone, but no, the computer clock time was not frozen. She was meeting Dan right after work, so needed to leave on time, and not stay late to review the presentation she'd already reviewed three times one more time. She skedaddled out of work the exact second her desk monitor said 5:30.

The weather was warming up outside, so the quick walk down to the mall to the museum was just long enough that she opted to metro one stop and limit the amount of time she spent in the humidity. Her hair was stick- straight most days, but still able to absorb amazing amounts of humidity and expand.

That was part of the reason she had given up on finding another outfit. Short of changing in the museum bathroom, whatever she wore was going to be a little damp. Also, nothing in her closet seemed to say, I sure hope this is a date, but if not I guess we could just be friends, but perhaps friends that kiss? Anyway, Dan had seen her in ratty yoga pants, this was still a step up.

She paused on the steps of the museum. She refreshed her lipstick and ran her fingers through her hair.

She made her way inside, and through the bag check. Pausing by the mammoth that looked smaller than in the photos on the website, she checked her texts.

Dan had suggested meeting over by the entrance to the mammal exhibit.

She found the sign and made her way past clumps of tourists taking selfies with the mammoth. And there he was. She felt a buzzing along her skin, as if the barometric pressure had shifted. Dan wore jeans and a t-shirt and the shirt fit snugly but not tightly in a way that made her wonder if making soup somehow counted as an excellent workout regimen.

"Hi," she said.

"Hi." He smiled and reached out a hand. "Don't want to lose you in the crowd."

Amy took his hand and tried not to think too much about how warm, and soft, and yet callused his hand was. She wanted to explore his hand, and yet they were here to see - something. She had looked up all the exhibits earlier and now couldn't remember a single one.

"So, where did you want to start?" she asked.

"How do you feel about bees?" Dan asked.

"Are they going to be crawling on me?" Amy asked.

"No," Dan said.

"Then fine." They went upstairs to the insect zoo. Dan led her to the different stations, showing her different exoskeletons, explaining the different types of bugs and bees. "How often are you here?" she asked.

His enthusiasm was adorable. If he didn't already have three jobs, she'd suggest he should also work here.

"Oh only once or twice year. There are so many museums. This one is popular with kids they get a lot of large groups in the spring and summer. So, I try to hit the lighter periods."

"Makes sense," she said.

"Okay, we're up near gems if you want to take a look at that?"

"Is it just jewelry?" Amy found the jewelry parts of museums often boring. Yes people used to be super rich and spend a lot of time worrying over jewelry. It was hard for her to separate these exhibits from the obvious parts of who mined those jewels, who cut those jewels, under what circumstances were people today trying to acquire sparkly things to prove their wealth. Reality took away from the glitter.

"Let's take a look." Dan led her through, they moved quickly through the darkened mood lit rooms housing back lit jewels on display and into a narrower room with stacks of labeled rocks. Uncut hematite, green quartz, every kind of rock she'd ever heard of and plenty she hadn't. Dan kept hold of her hand but didn't push or pull her, letting her set the pace as they moved through. Back in the hallway, Amy's stomach growled.

"So that answers what next," Dan said kindly.

Amy laughed. "I guess it's time for food." The museum had a cafe but it was small, and so they walked north a few blocks to where there were a few fast casual places. Amy still intended on buying the food, but figured it would be easier if they picked a place where the bill wasn't high enough for Dan to put up a fight. They grabbed their trays and sat down in a corner table near a window.

They focused on their food, the silence companionable. Amy realized she had never actually asked if Dan was dating anyone or like even if he was into girls.

She supposed kissing him would be one way to get an answer, but probably she should wait until they finished eating.

DAN FOUND WHEN COUSINS and folks visited, they wanted to do the touristy stuff. Museums counted as a touristy thing that was just as fun for locals. Some things like going to the Ferris wheel at National Harbor in Maryland, or touring the Capitol were more of the I did that once and now I never have to do it again type thing.

They finished their food. The clock in Dan's head alerted him sleep and rest were calling to him, even if the sun was still up. When the chefs at the sandwich truck rolled in to the commercial kitchen two hours later than him, he sometimes wondered why he had decided on something with so much prep time. But he loved soups, and there had been a gap in the market. You could buy soup in DC, of course. And some food trucks included soup as an option. But no dedicated soup truck. The opportunity aligned with his skillset. But he missed sleep.

"I should probably get going," he said.

"Oh, yeah, sure." Amy gathered up her tray, and they got their trash taken care of.

Standing outside on the sidewalk he hesitated over what to do. Amy leaned in and kissed him. He froze for a second, checking if this was a dream, that any moment he would wake up and find this wasn't real. He placed his arms on her hips and shifted, licking, tasting, learning the way her lips, and tongue felt against his, her body felt pressed against his. He wasn't dreaming because his dreams had never been this good.

She broke the kiss, "I probably should have asked first. You're not seeing someone right?"

Dan shook his head, still dazed.

"Me neither. I probably have like terrible timing. You need to get sleep and I can't be held responsible for you falling asleep in your truck tomorrow."

Dan nodded. Everything Amy said was sensible and smart. And he hated all of it. He wanted nothing more than to kiss Amy more, touch her more, and find some non-public place together. He felt ready to take on the world. Thinking through his schedule he was dismayed to realize Saturday afternoon was the next gap of time he had. "Saturday afternoon?"

Amy pulled out her phone. "Yup."

"Okay." He leaned in a kissed her again, still thrilled that this was a thing he was now able to do. Leaning his forehead lightly against hers, he said, "I promise it is only an overblown sense of responsibility making me walk away now."

Amy smiled. "I know." She shimmied her hips gently against him in a move that was delightfully torturous. Yeah, he supposed his, ahem, feelings were pretty obvious.

He kissed her quickly and turned and walked away, resisting the urge to look back. It would just take her smile to have him rethinking all his priorities, and he couldn't.

Chapter 10

Amy: Saturday seems very far away.

Dan: Agreed.

Amy: Does Bull Lion having a kissing in the food truck policy?

Dan: Bull Lion generally has two people in the truck - it is never private in there. And I'm pretty sure anything beyond kissing counts as a health code violation.

Amy: Are you saying all those movies about chefs screwing in the back room lied to me?

Dan: No, I'm saying movie chefs don't have health code inspectors. But I've worked in kitchens, and bars, I would never say nothing has ever happened.

Amy: Have you ever???

Dan: No. Backrooms have uncomfortable shelves, tripping hazards, and even if you lock the door, someone will kick it in to get more flour or whatever.

Amy: Have you ever walked in on anyone?

Dan: Once. After that I got better at avoiding pantries when I'd just seen to giggling folks slip inside.

Dan: That never happens at offices?

Amy: Oh it definitely does. Like I haven't here. The place I worked at before, we could have been a soap opera the way folks were always hooking up and all that.

Dan: I'm relieved to know all those stories porn had told me are true.

Amy: I wouldn't say all. Like, I've never found anyone in the copy room. But offices, bathrooms, stairwells, yeah, they have seen things. As have whoever watches the tapes of the office cameras.

Dan: Office have cameras?

Amy: Oh yeah. Not true in kitchens?

Dan: Not usually on the kitchen side.

Amy: Interesting.

Amy: Okay, I should let you sleep. Thanks for showing me the museum. And the kissing part was good too.

Dan: You think saying that is going to help me sleep?

Amy: I feel like that is an incriminating question that I would be a fool to answer. Sweet dreams.

Chapter 11

Amy tried not to tap her feet as she waited for the tea she had ordered. A new package of condoms sat in the inside pocket of her purse, just in case. She had hopes, of course, hence the condoms. She hoped for kisses, and touches, and learning more about Dan's skin. She'd seen and tasted the incredible care he put into his food. She hoped he showed that same attention to detail, that same enthusiasm she had seen in the museum, for other things.

The coffee shop was near the farmer's market. Amy had arrived early, in case Dan managed to pack things up sooner than expected. She had cleaned her apartment that morning and sitting there watching the clock trying not to make any new messes had gotten ridiculous.

She had managed three sips of her tea without spilling, when she felt like the air started to buzz. Dan walked in and immediately scanned the shop for her. She smiled and waved and tried to maintain her smile even as his answering smile did things to her insides. She felt warmer and wanted to shiver.

He ordered a drink and came over, leaning over to kiss her before he sat. The kiss quieted her worries while sending her brain off in the direction of far more interesting images. But first they needed to talk. Or something.

"How did the market go?" she asked.

"Good. We had a gazpacho that was popular, so we'll play around with that."

"Oooh, I like gazpacho. Are you going to do that on the truck?"

"We'll see, Mateo wants to, but it's easier at the farmers market where we have a little space for all the coolers we need. The truck has some refrigeration, but most of our equipment is designed to heat soup, not chill it."

"Ah," Amy said.

"Sorry, I spend a lot of time thinking about logistics and it is not always scintillating conversation."

"No, it's fine and I asked. You're running a small business, of course it takes up a lot of your time. And your brain." That was enough talking, right? Amy took a breath. "Not to be selfish, but what time do you need to get up to prep tomorrow?"

"It's a later market, so six."

Amy slumped. "I don't even know how you're alive. That's late?" Amy shook her head. "Not the point. Okay, so we have -" she checked the time on her smartwatch, "fourteen hours. I assume sleep needs to happen somewhere in there. Probably dinner too. I assume we're going to do that somewhere not in public, yes?"

"Yes." Dan leaned on the s.

Amy tried not to shiver. Again. She was used to dating someone who traveled a lot, so this wasn't a particularly long period for her to go without sex. She had discovered apparently once her sex button had a date, a timeframe, it had grown used to revving into overdrive. Her skin tingled, her body felt warm and wet, and so, so ready.

"So, my place or yours?" she asked.

"Mine is really tiny. And not very clean at the moment."

"Is yours closer to where you need to be tomorrow?"

"Yes."

"Let's do that then." Amy stood and grabbed his hand. "Lead the way."

DAN REGRETTED NOT CLEANING his apartment last night. He didn't know why he hadn't thought of it. Okay, he had thought of it. But he had been so zonked after going shopping for the ingredients for the gazpacho, that he had just fallen straight into bed. He wasn't really sure when the last time he had changed the sheets was. Definitely this month. Beyond that he couldn't swear to anything.

They got in the car. Dan looked over at Amy. "My place is in the basement, so not the best light."

"Hey, Dan," Amy said.

"Yeah?"

"Not planning on painting, okay. So don't worry."

He reached over and squeezed her hand. He parked and then led her around to the side to his entrance.

He opened the door, kissed Amy quickly and said, "Just five minutes?"

"Okay, but I'm timing you." She tapped her smartwatch.

He raced inside. He ran through and gathered as much discarded clothing as he could off the floor and stuffed it in the laundry hamper.

Peeking in the bathroom, nothing looked atrocious. He turned scanning the place as Amy walked in and shut the door behind her.

"Was that really five minutes?" he asked.

She stripped off her sundress in one smooth motion, tossing it on the floor. "Is that really what you want to ask right now?"

"No." He stripped off his shirt, also tossing it on the floor. His shoes and pants went next. Amy's bra was gone, and he stepped closer to her, watching as she shimmied out of her underpants. She stood back up, and he slid his arms across her back, pulling her in to kiss her.

Her hands moved over his back, and he slid his down hers, groaning a little as she tipped her hips against his. He still had his underwear on, but saw no reason they needed to be upright when there was a bed. He tugged her towards it, indicating she should climb on.

He followed, leaning in to kiss her mouth, propping his elbows on each side of her. "Hey, if I do anything that feels odd or weird, tell me, okay?"

"Yeah," Amy said her voice breathless. "Um, you too, right?"

"Right." He skimmed his hands over her breasts, noting what made her breath catch, what made her huff. His hands trailed circles over her stomach, her hips her thighs. Her thighs widened, and he shifted, teasing the inside of her thighs with his thumb, then stroking across her labia, pressing gently on her clit. He slid a finger inside her, pressing up, and watching as her breathing changed again. Keeping his finger stroking inside he leaned down and sucked her clit. Her breathing shifted and her hips pressed up. He increased the rhythm of both his mouth and his finger as her thighs tightened, and she shattered around him.

He wanted more already, but patience would be his reward here. He was sure he could spend the rest of his life making Amy come and be happy.

Chapter 12

Amy's sex button had been well and truly pushed. When the shimmers slowed, she reached down and tugged Dan up, kissing his lips, and tugging at his briefs. She wanted them off, she wanted him inside her, she wanted to feel him come. And she wanted to come again.

"I brought condoms." Her purse was near the entrance. His apartment wasn't big but right now that seemed very far away.

"I have some." Dan hopped off the bed, and dug underneath, revealing a box. He showed her the expiration date. "Still good."

"Excellent, let's get it on. Oh, you know what I meant."

His smile made parts of her clench in delicious anticipation. "I do," he said.

He rolled the condom on and got back on the bed. "You want on top?" he asked.

Amy did. They shifted so she could straddle him, could slide him slowly inside her, felling her body pulse around him. She paused, savoring the feel of him inside her, and partly wondering. Would he let her wait like this? Had he given up control only to take it back. But he seemed to have patience or maybe trust in her. He stayed still, though she could feel his thigh muscle twitch. She tightened around his cock and he moaned. She smiled, and rested her hands on his shoulders as she began to move, shifting her hips so he slid in and out, feeling, hearing their bodies move together and apart. She moved faster, her orgasm building inside her. As she shattered, she kept her hips moving, until his shudder told him he had finished too.

She stilled. Her whole body felt warm and her thighs felt like jelly, but she also wanted to do that like six more times. Her brain was ready to check the time, calculate how many orgasms they could fit in their time remaining. She was already worried it might not be enough.

Dan wasn't going to hop on a plane, he wouldn't be six or seven time zones away. Tomorrow morning he was going to get up early and go do something that wasn't her. The more things changed, the more they stayed the same.

But that was a tomorrow problem. Right now, she was definitely on a mission to have at least three more orgasms.

Chapter 13

After the farmer's market Sunday, Dan changed gears and did some ridesharing. Sunday afternoon wasn't as huge a time as Friday and Saturday night, but it was steady.

The number of rides slowed in the late afternoon. Dan stopped and dropped some soup with a small corner store that had just opened. Next, he intended to go straight home and rest. Sleep had been a little lacking the night before, and he should definitely get some before the week started. He knew that.

Dan: Hey, are you at home?

Amy: Is this the late afternoon version of you up?

Dan: That sounds like an incriminating question. I wanted to bring you some soup, but if you're not home, I can get it to you some other time.

Amy: I'm on my way home, how close are you?

He leaned against his car.

Dan: Ten minutes, but I'm not in the car yet.

Amy: Okay, I probably need twenty, but totally understand if you need to get home and rest.

Dan: I can be patient.

She sent back a smile emoji.

Some of the leftover summer squash soup was part of his dinner tonight, but there was enough for Amy too.

Seeing five minutes had passed, he slid in to the car. He could drive slowly.

He arrived and pulled into the spot. Checking his phone, Dan was a few minutes early, so he figured he'd wait before texting to see if she'd made it back.

"Hey, there."

He turned and there she was. In another sundress that made him want to help her peel off. Focus. He needed to focus.

She leaned in to kiss him and he met her, sliding an arm around her waist, trying to remind himself that sleep was important.

"So," Amy said, "you had soup?"

"Summer squash. It's another one that looks kind of like a smoothie." He handed her the small paper bag with the soup.

"Do you have time to come inside?" she asked.

"Sure," his mouth said even as his brain said, no you don't, go home and get to sleep.

But he followed her into the building and up to her apartment. She walked to the fridge and placed the bag of soup inside on a shelf that didn't look to have much other food.

"How much time do you have?" Amy said.

"Not much." He pressed against her, bracing his hands on the fridge and kissed her. Realizing he had kind of trapped her, he pulled back, "Sorry."

"Don't be." She tucked her hands just inside the back of his waistband, pressing her hips into his. He slid his hands underneath the hem of her dress, sliding up her thigh, stroking over the center of her underpants, gratified to hear her moan.

"May I?" he asked.

"Please," she said.

He slid a hand inside, stroking inside her. Her fingers tightened on his butt and then she came, squeezing his fingers, pulsing around them.

"Well, good thing I got that soup in the fridge." Amy kissed him and her fingers slid a little further inside his cargo shorts. He was hard as a rock, but as much as parts of him were convinced he could come inside her quickly and then leave, he knew he would be unable to tear himself away. He had already stayed out longer than he should have. "I want to stay," he said, "but I really have to go."

She followed him to the door, kissing him one last time.

It was worth the lost minutes of sleep. Even if he hated having to leave.

Chapter 14

Amy: Are you asleep yet?

Amy: Also, I assume you don't answer texts when you are sleeping, so if you are asleep, I am not expecting an answer and I'm sorry I bothered you.

Dan: I was asleep, sorry.

Amy: Don't be sorry. I miss the truck being nearby so I could see you at lunch for a bit at least.

The truck had scored coveted lottery slots this month, but none were near Amy's office building.

Given how things had gone when Dan had dropped off soup, he was pretty sure this was just as well. Except now he wanted to bring her soup tonight. Not a euphemism. Not really. If Dan created a neural link between soup and sex, things might get uncomfortable. Hostile workplaces probably didn't mean if it was you and your own sex thoughts stuck together, but focus was important when dealing with hot liquids. Losing focus could lead to scars.

Amy: What time do you get home tonight?

Dan: Probably six.

He had some food shopping to do, and then he'd be set.

Amy: Can I invite myself over to your place for a set time, if I promise to leave even if I have to slide out of there naked to do it?

Dan: I promised not to dump you naked on the sidewalk.

The weather was warm, but the neighbors might not enjoy it. Or might enjoy it too much.

Amy: I appreciate that.

Dan: You remember how to get there?

Amy: I do.

Dan felt a surge of energy as he pulled up and saw Amy sitting in the sun, the back of her head visible as she sat on the steps that led down to his apartment.

He hopped out of the car and cut across the lawn. She turned and smiled at him and he once again had to chant, sleep, priorities, money, to remind himself that he couldn't just bask in her for the foreseeable future. It had been days, literal days, since they'd moved from more than friends, but it already felt inevitable. Dan was used to long projects that took years to come to fruition. Nothing had ever worked out for him this fast. But those were thoughts for later, for now, he had a girl to get inside.

AS PROMISED AMY DRAGGED herself out of Dan's place exactly one hour after arrival. Okay, there were like two extra minutes of goodbye kisses, while her whole body buzzed, tingling, in a post orgasm kind of way.

Her phone buzzed. She fished it of her purse, wondering if it was Dan.

Lillian: Hey, I haven't seen you in a bit. Dinner Friday?

Dan was working at the bar Friday. Since he would want time to nap or eat after wrapping up the food truck, they had made plans to see each other Saturday after the farmer's market.

Amy: I'm in.

She got down to metro platform and checked the next train time before pulling up her calendar app. Oh weird. Friday was her birthday. She had a big presentation at work, the first one she was leading herself in this new role, so she had been red lettering the day in her brain and hadn't even made the connection.

Growing up the eldest of seven, there was not really money for things like birthday parties. Amy had done her best to try and make the day fun for each of her siblings. Their mom, it wasn't that she didn't care, she just didn't always have the time or emotional bandwidth for birthdays.

As an adult, Amy had kind of let it slide. She didn't get that excited about birthdays or any celebration centered around time. Surviving didn't seem worthy of celebration to her.

Amy wasn't a birthday Scrooge, if other people wanted to make a big deal about their birthday, they were allowed. She would happily show up and toast them. She just didn't want a big deal made of her birthday.

It was one of the few things she had put her foot down with Ryder on. Of course he wanted to make birthdays a big deal. He wanted to invite all his friends. Had gone so far as to throw a surprise party for her once.

She had walked out. Told him he wasn't allowed to decide what was important to her. And after that, he had acquiesced.

Of course then the rest of their social life started to become like that surprise party. He'd get home and Amy would want alone time with him. But he would want dinner out first. Just a few friends. Just a few friends was what he always said, whether it was three or twelve. They would have sex back at their apartment. He would grab his phone before the sweat had cooled, texting others, making plans for all the friends he needed to cram in whatever time he had before the next flight, the next disaster, or even the next conference where he would talk about disasters.

It wasn't just the travel, Amy realized. Dan's schedule was similarly as packed. But he was open to keeping time with her a priority, even if it wasn't the only priority. Amy had a job and bills and a passion for her work. She understood she couldn't be number one every minute of every day.

Of course, as she exited the metro train, it was probably too soon to be making grand pronouncements about the state of anything. She and Dan had been sex buddies for less than a week. Way too soon to know how things would actually play out.

As she walked down her block her phone rang. Ryder. Had she conjured him up?

"Hi," she said.

"Hey," he said. "Surprise."

Amy realized she could hear Ryder not just through the phone. He shifted out of the shadows. He was here in the flesh.

RYDER: HEY, DUDE, I'M in town. We should get together."

Dan: In town like DC?

Ryder's home base was still Philadelphia. Ryder's office was still based there, and he had sent pictures of the small place he'd gotten there after Amy moved, so they could try to see who had the smallest apartment. Of course, Ryder's apartment was small because Ryder traveled so much, he normally was in hotel rooms of various size and shape. Dan's apartment was small because any extra money was going into the truck business.

Ryder; Yeah, dude, staying with Amy.

Dan typed oh and then thought that that probably wasn't the correct response. Cool seemed wrong. Possibly the English language was fully unable to encompass the complex levels of feelings he had about this new development. He tapped his fingers against the fridge door. He had been pondering getting a snack before bed, but now turned to lean against the fridge.

Dan: It will be great to see you.

He desperately wanted to text Amy. Maybe Ryder had shown up and Amy was too nice to send him away all the way or maybe Amy and Ryder were never really broken up and Dan was a fool for not clarifying that sooner. If Ryder was at her place, she probably couldn't text freely about whichever of these situations was in play. He was going to have to dig down and find the patience he had been so sure he was good at. The skill that had gotten him through three kitchen jobs, through supplementing income with ridesharing and bartending, through studying in the early hours of the morning to make sure he understood everything he needed to for food certification. It had taken him three years to get here. He could give Amy some time to explain the situation.

Chapter 15

Ryder: Dinner tonight with some friends, babe?

Amy desperately wished she could return to her strategy of hanging up on Ryder. She hadn't hung up on him every time he called, but any time he wanted to do an after action on their relationship she had made liberal use of the call end button.

Ryder had not taken the hint that some time and space was still called for. He had instead decided he should show up and he could hang out with both her and whoever else he knew in town. On a Thursday. Because Ryder's job was not constrained by things like work weeks, he sometimes forgot that other people's were. Ryder was better at building communications apparatus than he was at actually engaging in human communication.

That was unfair. Amy liked Ryder. She didn't want to get back together with him, no way in hell. But he was a fun guy with fun stories.

Ryder: Have you checked into a hotel?

She opened up her text chain with Dan and hovered over it. She needed to talk to him and she wasn't sure she could properly explain what was going on in less than sixty-two texts. And he was working.

Amy: Hey, we should talk."

As soon as she hit send, she realized how that sounded. He would think she wanted to see less of him not more.

Amy: Ryder showed up but we're not back together. And I want to not be having this convo over text. So, let me know when is a good time. Sorry to bug you during the workday. Hope you sell lots of soup.

Hope you sell lots of soup? Terrible closer. But it was already too many texts. She'd be lucky if he didn't block her after all that.

"Amy, you have a visitor," Faith said, leaning in her doorway.

Was Dan here? No—the dude with the visitor tag on was Ryder.

"Hi, Ryder, what are you doing here?" Amy asked, keeping her voice polite, since the office walls were very thin. Why would he be here? Now? Ever?

Chapter 16

"Thanks, Faith," Amy said. She shut the door behind Ryder. "Ryder, it's not appropriate for you to show up at my office."

He looked confused. "I know you don't always check your phone at work, and I wanted to see if you had time to grab lunch."

Amy prioritized her complaints. She had just texted Ryder, so obviously she was checking her phone today. But that wasn't the point.

He had shown up last night with nothing but a bag and a smile and of course the overwhelming assumption that he was staying with her. She had let him in figuring they could have the conversation inside about how he was leaving. Because he had been traveling, and waiting, and while none of that was her fault, she felt she could at least offer him some water and a seat while he called around for a place to stay. He had fallen asleep on her couch. Had still been asleep when she left for work. She didn't have time to drag him out the door and still make her 8:30 meeting, so she left him, texting him he needed to find a place to stay. She was not accepting unannounced guests. So now he was unannounced at her office.

Amy checked, the time. They were going to lunch. They could have this discussion away from all the other ears in the office. She sent a quick email to her team that she was heading out for lunch and would be back in time for the presentation run through. She wasn't willing to let Ryder derail her day, but she also hoped more time now would save them more time later.

"Let's go," she said, grabbing her purse.

Ryder slid his arm around her waist in the elevator. She grabbed his hand and removed it, taking a step to the side.

They went to the sandwich shop around the corner. It was fast and the right amount of noise so if one of her coworkers showed up, they probably wouldn't be able to eavesdrop without standing right next to them.

One seated with their food, Amy put her hands on the table, not sure if it was for support or to keep her from doing something more drastic with them.

"Ryder, you have to stop treating me like your girlfriend. We are broken up."

"I know," he smiled, "but we're still friends, right?"

"That depends," Amy said. "You seem to think being friends means you have unlimited access to my time and my apartment, the one I pay all of the rent on. So, is that your definition of friends?"

"Oh Amy, you and your rules. Being friends doesn't have to have rules." Ryder took a bite of his sandwich.

A band tightened around Amy's chest, and she held herself back from kicking the chair. It wasn't the chair's fault. Amy's childhood had been an exercise in her mom making decisions they all had to live with. As the oldest, the other siblings looked to her when mom didn't make it home for dinner, when they needed to figure out how to get school supplies. Her mom's boyfriends, until Travis, had not taken on enough responsibility to be reliable, had never provided the stability for their mom to quit more than one job.

When she tried to talk to her mother, Indie would say to remember who was the parent here. Amy had exploded once, saying sure, if Indie was the parent, cool, then why was Amy feeding and shopping for these kids?

Her mom had gone steely. Reminded Amy that her money paid for the apartment they lived in and if Amy thought she was ready to handle that, then she would happily hand the bill to her.

Amy had backed down. Gotten herself college admission, financial aid, and one-way plane ticket out of there.

It had taken Amy until just now to realize that these patterns she had gotten into with Ryder echoed that. She had accepted less than what she wanted from him because she was used to only being able to get part of what she wanted.

"So, Ryder," she said, "since you don't have your bag with you, is it fair to assume you have found another place to stay tonight?"

"Fine, Amy, I'll stay with Dan or someone."

"Dan's place is tiny. Also he has to get up early."

"I'm sure it'll be fine. We used to share a tent." Dan gave her an assessing look. "Have you been to Dan's place?"

Amy hadn't even seen that landmine coming. She could tell Ryder of course. But was Dan cool with that? Was she? Would Ryder be gracious or sulky? Feeling a little like a contestant given a limited time to come up with the correct answer, she tilted her head. "You introduced us, remember?"

Ryder looked down at his sandwich very intently.

They were going to focus on the housing aspect. "Ryder, do you need help finding a hotel or an Airbnb?" She checked her watch. She still had time before the run through.

Ryder sighed and opened up his phone.

Keeping her phone in her lap, she texted Dan.

Dan: Hey, I have told Ryder he should not stay with you because your place is tiny and you get up early. Hope I didn't overstep there. He's finding a place to stay.

She and Dan were banking up a lot of things they needed to discuss. In person. So, Saturday. She could make it to Saturday.

"I found a hotel room I could use points for, happy?" Ryder said.

"Thrilled," Amy said with a small smile. "Now, I need you to solemnly swear that you are not going to show up at my office or apartment unannounced again."

"Will a blood oath be enough?"

"I have to eat here. No blood please," Amy said.

Ryder rolled his eyes and held up his hand. "I Ryder solemnly swear that though my travel schedule is unpredictable I will not show up at my friend Amy's apartment or place of work -," he tilted his head at her, "anywhere else?"

"That seems like a good list for me. You can talk with your other friends about their rules."

"Not everyone thinks friendship has rules."

"They really do, Ryder. Not everyone has to constantly remind their friends what the rules are. Okay, I am going to head back to work. I will meet you at five thirty to let you in to grab your stuff. Does that work for you?"

"Sure," he said. "I can hang out here though."

Amy started to tell him he was in a city full of museums, of people, of things to do that were not sitting in a chain sandwich place. But she was not in charge of Ryder having a great time.

She stood and left, taking the sandwich she still hadn't gotten a chance to eat with her.

Chapter 17

This spot near L'Enfant Plaza had rocking business, and it was a new batch of office workers to introduce Bull Lion to, so Dan was on his A game.

Both hot and cold soups, especially those that looked like smoothies sold well here, and the chicken ginger was always a hit, but some of the other heartier soups had been less successful. He wondered if that would shift as they headed into fall. This whole first year involved lots of data gathering. Their point of sale system let them track the sales, so he had spreadsheets and charts he could take a look at.

But the data gathering concerning him today was Ryder and Amy. Ryder often showed up without warning. DC and Philly were close enough together that he often dropped in for a day or two usually without warning until he was already here.

When Dan finally checked his phone, the number of texts made him want to toss the phone into the chicken ginger. But of course he did not need to be paying for a new phone or ruining the remaining soup.

Technically, he knew Ryder was used to staying with a friend when he came to DC. Before Dan's dad had moved to Delaware for the beach life, Ryder had often stayed with him. Dan's own place was tiny, so sure, Ryder would have picked Amy's. If it wasn't farther away from the kitchen, Dan would be trying to have sleepovers there himself.

Scrolling through the texts from Amy, and then switching over to Ryder, Dan had a picture of what happened.

Ryder's texts started yesterday had started off positive. Ryder was always sure of his welcome.

Ryder: Staying with Amy, we should hang.

Ryder: Amy seems cranky, is the job stressing her out or something?

Ryder: Amy is being bossy about where I stay, so I'm going to be at the Camden tonight. They have a good bar there, we should hang. Or I can meet you wherever. I know you have to work too.

So, Amy had kicked him out. Dan couldn't help but smile. It didn't necessarily mean anything about her feelings for Dan, but it was certainly better to know she did not have any lingering feelings for Ryder. He had planned on having some sort of let's talk about our relationship conversation when they had hit two weeks, not wanting to jump the gun too much. He'd known for a while he wanted more with her, but didn't want to scare her off. Earlier today he wasn't even sure they were still on their way to two weeks. Now, he was much more confident.

"Look alive, dude," Mateo said.

Dan squinted at Mateo. "Was I looking dead?"

"Isn't that your friend?" Mateo pointed.

And sure enough, there was Ryder striding up the sidewalk. He looked great for someone who had to be jet lagged and travel weary. He didn't even look hot in the summer humidity. Dan had grown used to the heat. Working in kitchens didn't give you any choice. He wore clothes that kept parts of his body safe, he wore supportive shoes, just about everything in is life was practical and or functional. He had never figured out how to make his hair shinier, couldn't remember the last time he'd gotten it cut.

Dan wasn't used to thinking of himself in comparison to Ryder. They were different people. But he hadn't dated any of Ryder's exes before. It had only ever gone the other way around.

"Hey, dude," Ryder said, "the truck looks great. Oh hi," he nodded at Mateo, "you must be Mateo. I'm Ryder, I heard good things about you."

"Hi," Mateo nodded, "I follow your Instagram."

Dan glanced over at Mateo who shrugged.

"Aw, cool," Ryder said.

"Do you need soup, man?" Dan asked.

"I had a sandwich for lunch. What are you all up to for dinner? I'm meeting up with Amy, we should all go out somewhere. You must know all the best food places."

"I can recommend some places. Are you staying at the Camden near the museum or near Union Station?" Dan asked.

"Ah, Amy told you," Ryder said and his smile seemed knowing in a way that itched at Dan.

"You told me you were staying at the Camden," Dan said. Amy had said they needed to talk. He assumed based on the follow-ups she wasn't ready to tell Ryder about them. He was okay with waiting, but Ryder's smile was making him rethink that.

"Oh I did, right," Ryder said. "Yeah, I think it's the one near like Gallery Place.

"There's a good pizza place near there." Dan focused on the food. He wasn't in competition with Ryder after all.

"I like pizza."

"I'll text you the info," Dan said. "I may not be able to meet up with you right away, we have some shopping to do, but I'll definitely stop by."

"I can do the shopping," Mateo said.

Dan looked over at Mateo. "We'll talk."

"Okay," Ryder said, "sounds good. Amy wanted to meet at like five-thirty, but we probably won't get to the restaurant until like six-thirty so don't hurry on my account."

Dan smiled though his stomach burned a little. He had never noticed before how much Ryder talked about Amy like an appendage.

And he supposed Ryder probably had learned lots of wonderful things about Amy, he had dated her for a while. And Dan hadn't told Mateo or Xavier that Amy was wonderful, or kind, or that she was funny, or that he loved texting with her before he fell asleep.

Ryder and Amy had a history that was different from his history with Ryder, and that preceded his having any real knowledge of Amy. He fucking hated it. He was jealous of the time Ryder had had with Amy.

Of course, he realized as he and Mateo locked up the truck in the lot, there was one more thing. The more he learned about Amy, the more he realized it was easy to miss how deeply she felt things. Ryder not showing up for her likely wasn't the only reason they had broken up. Now that he knew Amy more, it broke his heart all over again that she had to go through all of that with only a virtual stranger to hold her hand.

It made it harder for him to think of Ryder the same way.

But that was a fight for Amy and Ryder to have, if she wanted to.

Dan: Hey, Amy, Mateo's going to do my shopping so I can meet you and Ryder for dinner. I suggested a pizza place near the hotel if that sounds good to you.

He hoped that told her enough that he wasn't worried or jealous, or not because he thought something happened. He was a little retroactively jealous of all the time Ryder had gotten with Amy. But once Ryder was back in Philadelphia, they could work on getting more time together, alone.

RYDER HAD GLANCED OVER at Amy a few times as she followed him into the hotel and watched him check in. She suspected he hoped she would change her mind about letting him stay.

The pizza place only had them wait ten minutes to get seated. Dan had texted that he was on his way, something Amy was both grateful for and terrified of. She felt like she had entered some sort of sitcom zone where you knew that by placing at the same table these people with a secret, there was no way that it would stay secret.

She didn't think there was anything wrong with her dating anyone this many months after she had broken up with Ryder. If she and Dan had any kind of warning about Ryder's arrival they could have talked about what it meant and if they wanted to tell him. It seemed unfair to Dan to make that choice without talking to him, and they hadn't had a chance to talk alone.

Seated at the table, Amy and Ryder looked through their menus. Amy had looked around. It was one of those places adorned with a lot of signs, so you could certainly keep yourself busy reading all the decor.

"So, how's your job going?" Ryder asked.

"It's going well," Amy smiled. "And it looks like you had some fires to deal with." Wildfires in California had been burning for some time.

"Yep. They've got in under control now, so I won't have to go out there again. Fingers crossed."

"Oh good." Ryder had tended to dislike fires. For fires his team arrived mid-catastrophe, whereas hurricanes, earthquakes, mudslides, they often arrived after the initial blast. It created a different kind of challenge.

"Have you had a chance to watch any TV?" Amy asked.

"Oh yeah, I watched this sitcom, 'Rolling Bridge' it's so funny, I think you would like it."

"Yeah, it's a good show." She had in fact told Ryder to watch it, even sat him down in front of an episode. But sometimes she forgot who she had watched things with too.

"Are you still reading?" Ryder asked.

Amy tried not to laugh. Small talk was hard, but she could swear that once upon a time she and Ryder had known how to carry on a conversation. "I am still reading. Got a non-fiction about charitable giving, and a romance."

"It's not that one about how all non-profits are evil is it? Because I met that guy, and he's and asshole. Besides, half the stuff in there was wrong."

"Hey, there," Dan said, "thanks for waiting for me."

"Hey, Dan." Amy was tempted to get up and kiss him for multiple reasons, including putting an end to a discussion of why the book she was reading couldn't possibly be right or useful just because Ryder said so. But she stayed in her chair, settled for smiling and nodding hello.

"Hey, man, good to see you again. Is Mateo coming too?" Ryder asked.

"Mateo is doing grocery shopping and then heading home. But he said it was nice to meet you."

"Oh," Ryder said, "I'm sorry he didn't join us. I would have loved to talk with him more."

Amy was confused. "When did you meet Mateo?" she asked.

"I stopped by the truck this afternoon. Wanted to take a look. It looks great, man" he said to Dan. "I'm glad you're living your dream."

"Thanks," Dan said.

"So what soup did you get?" Amy asked. If Ryder had told her he was going by the truck, she could have gotten him to get her some of the broccoli gazpacho. She really wanted to try some.

"Oh, I was full from the sandwich, so I didn't try any. But Dan's a great cook, everything he makes is great."

The waitress came and took their order. This saved Amy from wondering why Ryder thought bothering people at work was okay. She understood it was tough when you had a day off that others didn't. Heck she understood trying to make plans with Dan was tough, he had so many hours of his day spoken for. But once, just once, early in their relationship Amy had suggested she could come with Ryder and hang back at the hotel on one of his trips. He had gotten furious. These trips he took weren't vacations. He wasn't there to have fun or be a tourist. He was working. Amy had agreed. Had realized right after a disaster is often not the best time to visit any place. And yet, somehow he thought there was nothing wrong with showing up at both Amy and Dan's workplace. And he hadn't even bought Dan's soup.

After the waitress left, Amy turned to Dan. "Does Mateo often do the grocery shopping?"

Dan smiled. "This is a first. So we'll see how things look tomorrow. I asked him to text me pictures of the food as he loaded the cart and he accused me of being a micromanager."

"Ah," Amy said. "Well, I guess if Bull Lion's social media says vegetable medley soup tomorrow, I'll know why."

Dan chuckled. "Yeah, that's not what we have on the schedule so here's hoping all is well tomorrow."

"Schedules change, people will understand," Ryder said.

"They do change," Dan said, "but we are finding the government office folks are a little particular. So no matter how many times we post a change, someone will show up and be like, but Monday you said today would be squash, I wanted squash."

"Wow, life in retail," Ryder said, "I don't envy you."

"Well, I don't think I could travel as much as you do, so we're even," Dan said.

Amy smiled. Oh god. Oh gosh. Oh crud. She was torn between really wanting to see how this played out and really really wanting to talk about sitcoms again. Or sports. People liked talking about sports, didn't they?

Ryder laughed. "Yeah, not everyone can put up with this lifestyle." He winked at Amy.

Her face heated, and she could only hope her coloring plus the dim restaurant lighting kept it invisible to her table mates. Nope, she was not ready to have this conversation. It might take a decade.

Part of her wanted to stand on the table and tell everyone she was dating Dan. That part was smaller than the part of her that didn't want to make a scene. That didn't want to declare something Dan might not be ready to back her up on. That didn't want to put shoes on tables, because people ate there.

Amy grabbed her water glass and sipped, deciding silence was the better part of valor or something.

"So, how long you in DC for?" Dan asked.

"I had planned on a few days. I know it's tough for folks to make time for me when they have work to attend to. But we can all do dinner tomorrow right?"

Amy put the glass back down on the table, reducing the likelihood she would dump it over Ryder's head. Oh now he understood people had jobs. How fascinating.

"Dinner sounds good," Dan said "There's lots of museums. Some new ones since you were last here, and of course there will be new exhibits."

"Yeah, I might catch a movie or something. And there are some folks I can meet up with down near the White House."

And there they were. Less than twenty-four hours into a supposed vacation and Ryder turned it into a work trip. Ryder didn't believe in work hard play hard, when work hard and keep working harder was on the table. It was enlightening how a few months outside the direct sunlight of the Ryder sphere made Amy more aware of the lack of balance. Sleep was good, rest was good, sex that didn't have to be dependent on the whims of nature was good.

But hey, there was someone out there for Ryder too. Someone who loved that sunlight of his direct attention but only in small doses, because it was a lot. Amy had been that person herself for a while. She just wasn't anymore.

Their pizza arrived, per Ryder's suggestion, and they all swapped pieces so everyone could try each one. They were all good, and happy eating noises followed. The rest of the night they talked about fun things. Ryder told great stories about his travels. And they managed to find some mutually agreeable pop culture.

After dinner, they all three walked the two blocks to Ryder's hotel. Amy paused on the sidewalk outside the entrance. "I have a big day tomorrow, so I'm going to head straight to metro, but I can do dinner tomorrow."

"Oh, come on up for a second," Ryder said. "You guys should see this room."

"Sure," Dan said shifting closer to the hotel steps.

"I'm going to head home," Amy said with a smile, "but you two have fun. Good night." She hugged Ryder and then Dan and then waved and headed down the sidewalk.

DAN REGRETTED NOT LEAVING with Amy, or just leaving for that matter. Tomorrow he was working a shift at the bar. He was going to regret missing out on sleep. They went up and Ryder did a tour of the room.

"Here we have a bed, here we have what they call a desk, but it is really a glorified side table, and here is the bathroom. The shower water does get nice and hot though, which is always great."

This hotel room was slightly smaller than Dan's apartment, but because it didn't have a kitchen, it seemed more open. Dan supposed it helped when the person staying in it likely only had a week's worth of stuff. Dan had learned early on that having enough stuff so you didn't have to do laundry every day created interesting logistical challenges for keeping your place clean when you also didn't like putting away clothes.

"I like it, and the location is great," Dan said.

"It's little more fun than Amy's neighborhood."

Dan figured Ryder really wasn't aiming for a discussion of the changing neighborhoods in DC and the results of gentrification. So he nodded in what he hoped was a non-committal way.

"So you're planning to do some work tomorrow?" he asked.

"Yeah. We'll see. I'm not good at sitting around and waiting, you know? I thought Amy might be willing to take some time away, especially this week, but, I guess not. She can be a little cold about things."

Dan disagreed. Amy felt things deeply. And sure, sometimes she expressed that by employing an expression of ice, but she only needed the icy expression when things had hurt her.

He had planned to needle Ryder a little about the working in retail comment, but held back, knowing Amy was already on edge. Ryder meant well, but sometimes Ryder got a little full of himself, like he was out there saving the world one phone network at a time, and other people weren't. Ryder did important and useful work.

Feeding people was also important and useful work. The only difference was many people assumed the people who fed them deserved little, no benefits, minimum pay, and respect only if they were polite. Even though everyone had to eat. Even though eating food prepared by someone who didn't know what they were doing could actually kill you.

But Dan had quickly seen they couldn't have that discussion in front of Amy without Amy getting caught in the crossfire. Dan was used to Ryder blustering. Ryder either didn't know how to tell when he had hurt Amy or wasn't taking care not to do so.

"Well, if you need other ideas for things to do with you day, I have lots of suggestions."

"I'll be fine. It was good to see you. And we can do dinner tomorrow?"

"Sure. It might have to be quick. I'm working the bar too. We'll figure it out."

"Well, we can go with you to the bar. I'm sure Amy would love to see it too."

"She's been. Went with her friend Lillian." Dan could explain he had been ridesharing that night, but it seemed like not the point of the conversation.

"Well, maybe Lillian can join us too."

"Maybe," Dan said. The Lillian Xavier thing was also complicated and something Dan was trying to tread carefully with. Since everyone involved was an otherwise unattached adult he didn't see any reason to poke the bear so to speak. "But yeah. I'll head home and send you a list of suggestions. I know my dad is sorry he isn't here to put you up. He always loved having you stay with him."

"Yeah, I had forgotten he moved. He's liking the beach?"

"Loving it. My bet is he runs for city council or joins the library board by the end of the year."

"Wouldn't surprise me. Okay, head home dude. Don't worry about me. I know how to entertain myself."

"I know you do." Dan hugged Ryder and then walked out.

He texted Amy as he waited for the train.

Dan: Hey, I told Ryder I'm working the bar tomorrow but could grab dinner before. Mentioned you had been to the bar with your friend Lillian. Sorry if that's weird.

Her reply came immediately. Dan tried not to hope too much that maybe she'd been waiting to hear from him.

Amy: It's not weird. But it will help me connect the dots when Ryder tells me to bring Lillian.

Dan: It was good to see you midweek.

Amy: It was good to see you too. I wasn't keeping us from Ryder, btw. I just didn't want to make things weird without talking it through with you.

Dan: He's adjusting to a lot this trip.

Dan was not overly concerned with Ryder's ability to adjust to Amy dating anyone, including Dan. Ryder was his friend. Right now Dan was deciding if he should be grateful Ryder was just clueless enough to not be able to hold onto Amy and eternally grateful that Ryder held onto Amy just long enough to get her to Dan. Neither was a very evolved response. Ryder had been in a period of change for a while, heck so had Dan. Things changed, parents moved, jobs asked different things of you that you either committed to or walked away from. Amy and Ryder had probably worked until they didn't.

But Dan was hard-pressed to be sad about the current state of things.

Amy: Yeah, probably best to tell him some other time.

Dan's train arrived and he pocketed the phone. Because even though it aligned with what he was thinking, seeing Amy say it, made him feel lesser in a way he needed to think on.

The train ride home felt jerkier than usual. He was still queasy when he picked up his car to get the rest of the way home.

Chapter 18

Amy: Hey Dan, let me know when you get home.

Amy: You probably need sleep. No worries. Talk to you tomorrow.

AMY: SO, REMEMBER HOW we are meeting up tomorrow?

Lillian: Yes...

Amy: Okay, well, now my ex is in town and he's friends with Dan so they are both coming and please you cannot bail on me.

Lillian: Does the ex know about you and Dan?

Amy: No. Well, I mean I haven't told him. I haven't had a chance to talk to Dan without Ryder being there. I think he's already asleep. Dan. Not the ex.

Lillian: So I am the buffer now. Fun.

Amy: I know. I mean, I'm sure everyone will be nice to you. Ugh. I should have just told Ryder. But now it seems weird. I would rather tell him later. When he's like not in town. Is that terrible?

Amy: I'm sorry. I do not need you to solve my love life. But please come tomorrow.

Lillian: phrasing

Amy: Oh grow up. Please attend tomorrow. Are you happy now?

Lillian: Or...let your ex and Dan have dinner and we can go do something fun for your birthday.

Amy: Ugh. I mostly hate birthdays. Wait, did I tell you it was my birthday?

Lillian: Mind like a steel trap. We were talking star signs.

Lillian: After this dinner are we doing something fun or are you going to sneak off with your guy. I assume there is sneaking and that's why my buffer assistance is needed.

Amy: No sneaking. He's working at the bar, so we're having an early dinner before going off in separate directions.

Lillian: Okay, I am in. But you should also take a long lunch and go to the yarn store and get your birthday discount.

Amy: There's a yarn discount?

Lillian: Yes. This is why you should tell people these things.

Amy: I guess. Oh, and thank you on all counts.

DAN: LOOK AT THIS CAR I saw. [picture of sparkly purple car glistening in the sun.]

Amy: Wow! That is a statement. I kind of want that nail polish.

Dan: Also, sorry I missed your texts last night. I crashed when I got home.

Amy: I figured. We can talk tomorrow, I guess.

Amy: Oh, Lillian's coming to dinner with us tonight. I let Ryder know.

Dan: Cool.

Amy: Ryder will go back to Philadelphia tomorrow. And then we'll be back to normal. I mean, I know he's your friend.

Dan: Back to normal is good though.

Dan: You have your big presentation thing today, right?

Amy: Yes.

Dan: You'll be great. Purple car is a good omen.

Amy: Lol, thanks. See you at dinner.

Chapter 19

Ryder: What's National Harbor?

Dan: It's like an hour away. There are shops and stuff, and a Ferris wheel. Easiest to get there by car, although there's a ferry thing too.

Dan didn't see reply bubbles, so he pocketed the phone and finished checking the soup temperatures. The Friday lunch crowd tended to come earlier and come hard in this location.

"All the produce looked good, yeah, Chef?" Mateo said.

"I already told you everything looked good," Dan said. He wasn't clear why Mateo was so psyched to have gotten to grocery shop. Who was he to burst the guy's bubble.

"So, can I do it again?" Mateo asked.

"Actually, if you could do it tonight, that'd be perfect. I think we have enough stuff for the cannellini bean stew already, but if we need stuff for the pesto soup."

"Sure. I can come to the farmer's market too."

"I appreciate it," Dan said, "but I can't afford to pay you weekends too. Not yet."

"Got it. Just think on it, if you have friends in town or anything like that."

"I will. And I appreciate it."

"Hey, you two," Ryder said.

Dan turned. He hadn't noticed anyone walking up to the truck which was a terrible sign. He really needed sleep. He should add that to his shopping list.

"Hey, Ryder." They exchanged a handshake high five combo. Ryder also shook hands with Mateo.

"So, about that harbor. I had an idea."

Dan smiled. Of course Ryder had an idea. The only question was if Dan was going to regret knowing about this idea since it would eliminate the need for plausible deniability later.

"If I could borrow your car, I could be out there and back easily in time for dinner. I looked at the water taxi, and it has strict leave times so if I miss one, I'll be late by like an hour."

"My car is at the lot. You'd have to go get it." Dan had lent his car to Ryder before. Ryder was a good driver. Dan wasn't using the car today. It felt like unnecessary possessiveness to hold on to it when Ryder could use it. He didn't want to delve too deeply into the unnecessary possessiveness.

"No probs. I can gas it up and stuff too, while I'm there. And I have a travel app to warn me all the things."

"Okay, sure man. Let me text you the address of the lot. And the keys are here." He detached the car keys from his others. He reached for his phone. Patted his pockets, looked under the shelf, nothing. "Mateo, have you seen my phone?"

"Naw, chef. I actually haven't seen you use it all day."

A group of three stood right behind Ryder. "Okay, can you give Ryder the address info and I will talk to these nice folks behind him." Dan smiled and greeted the customers. He got soup orders going and Ryder waved as he walked away. Dan couldn't believe he hadn't noticed his phone was gone before now. He kept checking for it every time he opened a cabinet for another stack of soup cups, refreshed the compostable spoon containers. Once things finally slowed down, he and Mateo searched the truck. Dan also went through his morning.

He had definitely had the phone this morning since it was his alarm. He had texted Amy something at a stoplight on the way to the lot where the truck was parked. Had he dropped it getting out of the car? Hopefully he'd left it in the kitchen prep space. It was a shared kitchen so other people used it but everyone knew everyone so it would be there when he got back. If he'd dropped it in the parking lot, it was probably dust now, with all the folks rolling in and out of there on any given day.

He had suggested a place not too far from the bar for dinner, so he knew where to meet up with everyone. He had meant to text Ryder that he might be better off parking the car back at Dan's. Dan was going to have to hope that all went well. He did not have time to deal with DC ticketing anywhere in either his schedule or his budget.

Dan had agreed to Ryder's last request because the guy who'd been there when his family had been through hell had racked up a lot of goodwill. Now, Dan was in the awkward position of feeling grateful for getting to meet Amy. Feeling grateful Ryder had been just bad enough of a boyfriend that Amy had ended up single not long after arriving in DC. But he hadn't known how to say any of that yet. So he had just handed over his keys.

AMY, SADAMI, AND FAITH gathered in Sadami's office, clinking their paper cups of sparkling water. Amy felt on top of the world. The presentation had gone well. They wouldn't know the final status on the funding for another week or so, but for now they celebrated. Amy knew this was just one milestone, but she felt like she could relax, like they really liked her here, like she had made the right decision leaving Philly for DC.

"Happy hour?" Faith asked.

"Oh," Amy checked her smartwatch, "actually, raincheck. My friend's still in town, so meeting up with him and some friends."

"Mm-hmm," Faith said, "okay."

"Okay, before Faith creates a hostile work environment, I'll mention, I'm getting home to my dude also. But Monday happy hour."

"Fine," Faith said.

Amy grabbed her stuff. Lillian was standing downstairs in the lobby. "I hope you weren't waiting long."

"Nah, summer hours. Everyone's coming in early and leaving even earlier. So, we're having dinner with your ex and your new guy? How very modern," Lillian said in an exaggerated British accent.

Amy started walking. "We are having dinner with my ex and his friend who is also my friend."

"Right, right, I know." They made their way down to the metro platform. "So basically, that means I have four metro stops to get all the details."

"I told you about Dan."

"Mm-hmm," Lillian said. "Only the basics. Mateo says he's nice, but Mateo likes everyone. He makes you happy?"

Amy smiled. "He does. I mean, you're not wrong that we are basically like still counting things in days, and he has like three jobs..." Amy realized with a jolt she had fallen for yet another workaholic. "And then Ryder showed up. But yeah, it feels easy in a way that surprises me and yet is good."

Lillian patted her shoulder. "Good. Yay. All of that is good. There's nothing wrong with easy."

"Does this mean your thing that we are not talking about is easy or hard?" Amy asked. She immediately realized from Lillian's expression the double entendre she had made, and they both burst out laughing.

"But seriously, it's not a thing - thing," Lillian said. She shook her head. "Okay, well not everything I say sounds dirty. Basically, less relationship more mutually beneficial agreement that no one, meaning my brother, needs to know about because it's just a thing. And I'm not mentioning it to the other knitting ladies, because this city is too small, one of them will tell someone who will tell my brother. There are not enough degrees of separation."

"Got it." Amy nodded. And she also understood this meant Lillian was entrusting her with the info.

They came out of metro and made their way to the Italian restaurant that Dan had suggested. The street was townhouses, but small commercial signs and large picture windows indicated some had become retail or restaurants. They walked up the steps and inside to give their name to the hostess. The hostess sat them down and when the waiter came over for drinks, Lillian engaged in a long discussion of the extensive wine list, and she ordered a bottle. When the waiter left, Amy said, "The guys might want something else."

"Well, they can order something else."

Amy smiled. True. She checked the time. It was only just the time they had agreed on and there were no messages. She hoped nothing had happened with the truck today. She pulled out her phone. The truck's social media only showed pictures of the daily soups.

Ryder wasn't here either, but that surprised her less. If he was off talking to other emergency management consultants, he had probably lost track of time. Amy was used to making excuses, had stopped including Ryder in invites that involved hard start times like movies and theater or concerts. Ryder had once missed an entire concert at Wells Fargo Center. Not just the opening act, but the whole thing. Had texted as they were getting in the cars to head back if he should hop in a cab. "No," Amy had said.

When it hit twenty minutes, Amy texted Ryder, "Hey, are you on your way?"

She texted Dan, "Hey, do you want us to order something for you?" He was the one who had the tight timeline.

At thirty minutes and no response from either Ryder or Dan, Amy and Lillian had made enough of a dent in the bottle of wine that Amy was sure food was needed.

They ordered food, she and Lillian talked about TV, about knitting, about some of the other folks in their knitting circle, and various other things. Lillian didn't ask what had happened to Dan and Ryder once food arrived, but Amy could feel the pity. She was used to this feeling. This feeling where you were supposed to be joined by someone at a location and time that had been chosen to suit various schedules and needs. And then, after all that, no show.

Helping other people was a great excuse. It was every single time. Amy just wanted to know if it was okay for her to be mad, or sad, or hurt. Amy had been prepared to deal with the awkward of Ryder and Dan at the same table. Navigating one more night of not being able to communicate fully the state of things.

Somehow it had not occurred to her that she might be sitting here alone, if she hadn't begged Lillian to come along. That the thing that Ryder and Dan had in common, for all their apparent differences, was limited space for keeping non-work commitments. She had thought Dan's jobs all being in the same location, being relatively predictable would save her from moments like these.

If Ryder was on a plane somewhere, if Dan had some sort of unavoidable accident, or if they were both in an accident together, or if metro had had a meltdown, then sure. She could understand. She was an adult.

She leaned over and squeezed Lillian's shoulder. "I'm so glad you came out tonight."

"Thanks. And by the way, um, hope you don't hate this."

The waiter appeared with what looked like a very fancy ice cream bar, it had three different colors arranged in stripes and was covered with chocolate and hazelnut chunks. In the center was a candle. The waiter flicked a lighter on and lit the candle, gathering the other staff to sing "Happy birthday" to Amy.

She had so many memories of smiling falsely while singing over birthday cereal or some other thing she had told her siblings was totally a real birthday tradition. She had disabled her birthday on social media, finding random happy birthday messages felt hollow. The first year her mom had dated Travis, they had video chatted her with the two youngest siblings. Amy had been furious. Oh sure, now her mom remembered birthdays. So she had declared birthday moratorium.

But she didn't hate this. She smiled at the wait staff and it was real.

After the song, the waiter said, "It's a gianduja, so three gelato layers, and then chunks of chocolate and hazelnut. Enjoy." He placed two spoons down on the table.

Amy felt the tear rolling down her cheek before she even realized she was going to cry. The other eye joined in and she grabbed her napkin, trying to dab like she was worried about stray tomato sauce and not anything else.

"Oh, sorry, you hate it. Is it the attention or the dessert?" Lillian asked.

"No, I'm just emotional for some reason. But, thank you. And you have to help me eat this." She handed Lillian a spoon, taking a bite for herself. Oh it was good. Dan had great taste in food.

Ugh, Dan. Another tear slipped out, she caught it on a knuckle. She pulled out her phone.

Amy: Hey, Dan, hope everything's okay. I just can't keep doing this. Let's end this before it hurts more.

She thought about showing the screen to Lillian, making sure it wasn't birthday fumes, or more likely wine, but no, she needed to do this. What was it Lillian had said, mutually beneficial. Amy needed a relationship that was mutually beneficial and not just in bed. If Dan was hurt, then someone should have told her right? And if no one was going to tell her, then that meant something too.

Chapter 20

Dan was having a day. Or a night. He usually tried to stay away from such predictions when a bar shift still loomed ahead. Everyone in retail knew if you said something silly like it was quiet, you were cursing yourself. Calling things nuts, when the night was young was similarly unlucky. But things were definitely not good.

Traffic getting the truck back to the lot had been heavier than usual. Mateo had offered to take the truck back himself, but Dan needed to find his phone. He and Mateo had combed the kitchen and the parking lot. No luck. He realized he didn't have Amy's number memorized, so had Mateo text Ryder to let him know he was running late and to please pass that on.

Because Mateo couldn't text Dan from the grocery store, they went over in detail what was needed for tomorrow, double checking the inventory carefully. Dan then thanked Mateo who promised to stop by Bottom's Up and let Dan know how the shopping had gone. Dan was also going to need to figure out the whole phone situation.

When he got on metro and switched lines he got someone to check the time. Metro stations were like casinos sometimes, trying to figure out the time it was tricky unless you were standing at the kiosk.

When the dude he asked, said "Eight," his stomach dropped. He was in so much trouble. He should be at Bottom's Up already helping get things ready for open. He should have checked the time sooner. Amy and Ryder and possibly Lillian too had met early for dinner to accommodate his schedule and now he was going to stop in and leave immediately.

He raced up the steps to the Italian restaurant, scanning the small seating area as he checked in with the hostess. "I'm sorry sir, they left about fifteen minutes ago."

"Okay, thanks. You don't happen to know where they were going next."

She shook her head.

Okay, he raced back down the steps, doom rising from his stomach to his throat. He walked swiftly to Bottom's Up. "Hey, man, sorry, I'm late," he said to Xavier.

"It's okay," Xavier said, "Mateo gave me a heads up you had sort of a challenging afternoon. How was dinner?"

Dan started stacking glasses from the tub. "Oh, dinner, yeah, I didn't make it."

"Oh wow. You missed your girl's birthday too? You are having a day."

"Wait, what?" Dan couldn't have heard correctly. His chest felt tight, but he didn't want to drop a glass so he tried to ignore it.

Xavier raised an eyebrow at him, pausing in refilling the glass of their one early bird. Bottom's Up catered more to the late night, getting off shift crowd, although they had enough locals who showed up when doors opened to keep things going.

"That's what I heard. This dinner was a yay presentation and happy birthday."

"Oh shit," Dan said.

So now he had two additional problems. Because if Xavier knew it was Amy's birthday, and Dan didn't, what did that really mean for their relationship? Yeah, he'd been out of communication much of the day, but there were times all week she could have told him her birthday was happening. It was one thing for Ryder to know things about Amy that he didn't yet. But Lillian was newer to Amy's life than Dan was. Maybe Amy was colder than he had thought.

He asked if Xavier knew anyone he could text to pass the word that Dan was sorry for running late. Obviously they both knew who Dan was asking Xavier to text.

"That's the only message you want to send?" Xavier asked.

"Yep," Dan said.

"Okay," Xavier said. When he pocketed the phone, he added. "By the way, this is an exception. I generally do not have any way to contact your girl."

"Got it." It hardly mattered though. Amy clearly wasn't his girl.

LILLIAN VETOED GOING to her brother's bar even though it was close to the restaurant. "You should definitely go sometime without me, Circle is great. But nope. That's how I know how small things get. I used to hang out over at the Blue Spot. No one related to me worked there. Come to find out, the bartender there was dating the manager at Circle. It was too much. We should get to an entirely different neighborhood."

Amy's mental map of DC was still filling itself in. She let Lillian lead her into a rideshare, to headed away from the neighborhood with Xavier's bar. Where maybe Dan had made it to that commitment on time. The neighborhood her apartment in was not known for its nightlife, something she liked about it. But it did have a small bar about a block away she had been meaning to check out.

The rideshare got them there quickly, and she and Lillian found two spots along the counter. The first glass of wine was amazing, and Amy made note to start coming there more often.

Amy's phone buzzed, and she checked the readout on her smartwatch. The text was from Ryder. She pulled out her phone, things on the watch were a little fuzzy, possibly from wine.

Ryder: Hey, ran into some traffic on the way back. Let me know where to meet up with you guys.

She tucked the phone back in her purse and took another sip of wine.

"The ex?" Lillian asked.

Amy nodded.

"Well, let's toast to being wiser." Lillian held up her glass and Amy clinked it with hers, they both drank.

"I wish I was wiser," Amy said.

"You are," Lillian said. "Even when we repeat some patterns, we recognize them as patterns."

"Oh wow, you definitely are wise, Lillian." Amy looked at her wine glass. Lillian was either very wise, or this wine made everyone sound profound.

Lillian sat up straighter. "Thank you, in another year you'll probably be as wise as me. Of course, I'll be older and wiser too. So we shall see."

"Well, now I think we should toast to you, at such an advanced age still being like able to come out and drink."

Lillian pursed her lips. "Watch it, whippersnapper."

"Okay, I take it all back."

"Barkeep!" Lillian slammed her hand down on the bar. She then patted the bar as if to apologize for being harsh. "Sorry Danait, I know you have a name, but what do we say for a round of birthday shots?"

"Oooh, can anyone get in on that?"

Amy turned and there was her neighbor Helena. "Hi, Helena."

Helena slid onto the bar stool next to Amy. "I don't usually run into you here." She waved at Danait who smiled back. "Get them the good shots. On me,"

"Oh, you have to join us then," Lillian said leaning deeply on the bar so that she could see, Helena.

"Sorry," Amy said, "this is my friend Lillian, and this is my neighbor Helena."

Danait lined up the shots in front of them and and poured one for herself too. "Happy birthday," Lillian singsonged, and then they all tossed their shots back. It burned but in the way that was kind of fun and almost cleansing. Amy hoped it could banish the tears, the fears, the unnecessary worries about adults who didn't show up.

Chapter 21

Amy's phone would not shut up. She sat up, didn't see it next to her on the bedside table. There was a glass of water. She chugged it down. Her head wasn't too bad, but she felt slightly sticky, like her skin had been hard at work expelling alcohol through its pores, and now she needed a shower. Her phone was chirped again. The display on her smartwatch had gone nuts and just showed a giant number as if to say: Look, lots of people want to talk to you. You should get on that.

She found the phone in the pile of clothes she had left on the floor. She stuck the clothes in the hamper.

The texts went back several hours.

Ryder: Hey, I found Dan and he missed you too. Hope dinner was good. I leave tomorrow, would love to have breakfast with you before I go.

Ryder: Hey, Ames, you up for breakfast?

Ryder: Okay, well, I'm getting on the train. We'll try to plan better for next time. Hope you enjoyed your birthday.

Yeah, Amy noticed the we in we'll try there. As if him no-showing dinner after being relentlessly underfoot a day before was somehow a failure to plan. Well, it likely was, but Amy was sure it wasn't her failure. But, as Lillian said, older and wiser.

Amy: Have a safe trip.

Unknown: Hey, this is Helena, we are besties now, so you wanted my number in your phone.

Unknown: Okay, Lillian says she is claiming DC bestie. I get to be second bestie.

Unknown: Also I am supposed to remind you your plan is to make new mistakes this year. Happy birthday.

Unknown: Also Ms. Overgaard started vacuuming at seven. On a Saturday. I'm sure that's totally coincidental. Not her apartment. The hallway.

Unknown: Whoops, guess you might be sleeping through it. Kudos to you.

Amy switched back to Dan's texts.

Dan: Hey. I hear it was your birthday. Hope you were able to spend it with the people important to you.

What the hell was that? Why was he being all sad sack about no-showing her? She was the one who was hurt. It was her turn, dammit.

She tossed the phone back on the floor, somewhat satisfied at the bounce thud it made on her bedroom rug. Not as great as throwing it at the people who deserved it, but it would have to do for now.

Amy stumbled into the living room to find a pile on the couch. Oh, yep, that was Lillian, gently snoring. After showering, Amy wiped away the steam, and looked in the mirror. "Amy He Metcalfe, you," she pointed at her reflection feeling ridiculous, "are not in charge of other people's behavior."

She still felt off, but maybe from the lingering alcohol working through her system.

She made started the coffee make and sipped some more water while it was brewing.

"Hey," Lillian said. "Happy day after your birthday."

"Coffee?" Amy held up a mug.

"Yes please." Lillian scrambled up and grabbed a mug. Amy was using a laptop table as her kitchenette table, so there was only one chair. Lillian sat on the arm of the couch facing Amy.

"So, grand plans for the day?"

"Ryder's headed back to Philadelphia, and so I got nothing. Hydrating, but that's not like a whole plan. You?"

"My day is free. Do we want to grab knitting and head to the shop? Maybe after a little food. There's a great place not far from the shop that has good breakfast sandwiches."

"That does sound good."

"And we should stop by my place, if you don't mind."

"I love that dress, but yeah I don't mind."

Lillian looked down at the floral dress. "It looked better before I slept in it. But thanks for letting me bunk."

"No problem."

Lillian kept looking at her like she was trying to decide whether to say something. Amy was too tired to make her. So she kept sipping her coffee.

On metro to Lillian's place, Amy kept feeling itchy, sticky, something. They were talking about TV again, but Amy kept feeling it was a distraction, she just couldn't figure out from what.

At Lillian's, Amy sat on the couch and waited while Lillian threw on clothes. A process that seemed to involve some phone tapping. Lillian was probably talking to her dude who was not her dude. Amy hoped she hadn't done anything to interrupt or interfere with that.

Lillian came back out wearing a cute skirt and top. She sat on the edge of the couch and gave Amy a very serious look.

"So, I hate it when people butt into my life, so I swear I am just going to share some info and then stop. We can go back to talking about knitting or superheroes or whatever."

"Okay," Amy said slowly.

"Apparently, Dan lent Ryder his car yesterday, and he had left his phone in there, it had fallen under the seat, so Ryder didn't see it. Anyway, Ryder the car borrower went out to National Harbor and didn't account for Friday rush hour traffic, so was super late getting back. Meanwhile, Dan and Mateo ran into traffic getting the truck back. Dan didn't have your number memorized. And then I may have told Xavier it was your birthday, and maybe it seemed like Dan didn't know that."

"Oh," Amy said. "So, Dan's okay?"

"He's okay. And he got his phone back. Eventually."

"Good. You ready to go get breakfast?" She stood, needing to move.

Lillian nodded, and true to her word, she didn't bring it up for the rest of the day. Amy wished the same was true of her brain. It chewed on it. Worried on it. Theorized on it.

She guessed Dan's cryptic hurt was over her not mentioning it was her birthday. She definitely had meant to tell him. It seemed like hey let's have dinner and celebrate all these things, and then at dinner being like, and it's my birthday made sense for someone she'd known as long as she had Dan.

But maybe they were a big deal to Dan. She had known even when she sent him the let's end it text that he might have a good explanation. She was just tired of good explanations. Maybe she was wrong about who owed whom an explanation.

Lillian and Amy went to breakfast, and then to the yarn shop, where they sat down and took out projects. They knit and talked with others about things that were silly, things that were dirty, things that were fun.

The knitters were wonderful and along with knitting the brioche cowl, it kept her distracted enough that she could ignore the fact that the farmer's market would have closed. There'd be no texts from Dan about how things went. No plans made about how to spend the afternoon where he had some free time.

It wasn't loss of insider soup info Amy was mourning. Amy had been so proud of the progress she had made in setting clear boundaries with Ryder. But maybe she had set too many with Dan.

One of the things she had learned being with Ryder was that he didn't respond much to suggestions. She could suggest a restaurant sure. But if she tried to say, okay, I enjoyed that movie, let's do more things like that. Ryder would basically suggest another movie. It was fine. Ryder wasn't a mind reader. But Amy had skipped straight to late stage Ryder tactics and maybe hadn't spent time developing Dan tactics.

Crap. Amy He Metcalfe had screwed up. This was at least half her fault and possible more. So now she was going to have to figure out something new. Apologizing to Dan.

When it came time to head back home, Amy turned to Lillian. "Can I get something from you? Do you, or um, someone you know who is super not involved in this, have Mateo's number?"

Lillian nodded. "I can certainly see if I can get that for you."

"I appreciate it. Oh, and by the way, thanks for being a great birthday bud."

"Of course."

Amy waved to Lillian when she got off the train and stopped in front of Helena's door and knocked. Helena opened it, leaning against the door frame. "Aren't we supposed to text before we knock these days?"

"I need help figuring out how to apologize," Amy said.

Helena stepped back. "Come on in."

DAN HAD REACHED THE end of his smile. Working in food, he knew studies showed people bought food from happier food service workers when they had a choice. Farmer's markets were an exercise in food choice.

Mateo walked up to the table and Dan worried that he had lost his mind. "I told you I could handle things today, right?"

"You did," Mateo nodded. "However, I heard such excellent things," he had raised his voice to carry, "about this wonderful soup." In a more normal voice, he added, "Also, I hesitate to make predictions. But I feel like today, you might want someone to take the supplies back to the kitchen while you carry on with your day."

Dan's afternoon plans involved sleeping. Having gotten his phone back, despite the wobbly state of finances, he had decided sleep was the thing he needed most this afternoon. If it sounded suspiciously like wallowing, so be it. Besides, people wanted happy rideshare drivers. Okay, that wasn't true, but they wanted non-grumpy drivers. Dan just needed off time.

The bread vendor next to him started packing up, and he figured he could follow along. Since his stuff was prepared food, sometimes the people who showed up in the last five minutes of the farmer's market were more interested in him. But he was ready to stop.

He needed to call his dad. Talk to someone who considered him a person, not a bartender, not a boss, not an employee. He had Ryder for that too, but he was irrationally irritated at Ryder. Imagine having the world's technology available to you and being surprised about Friday traffic.

Ryder had returned the car in one piece, with Dan's phone. The phone had been on silent, and then eventually had powered down. So Ryder didn't notice he was driving around with an extra device, even as he texted it.

Other than the failure to plan for traffic, Dan knew none of the rest of the events of the night were Ryder's fault. So he wasn't talking to Ryder until he got over it. Ryder wouldn't notice, not because Ryder was careless, but more because Ryder's network of friends was so vast it was easy to pull back for a bit, and slide in when needed.

Dan supposed he should work harder on that for himself. He would add to the list of things he needed to do. Tons of cousins, former co-workers, church members and the like had showed up to support the food truck. But the number of them he felt comfortable saying hey, let's get a drink to was small.

Amy had - he looked away and back, no that was definitely Amy striding carefully towards him, balancing something in her arms. It was good to know hallucinating was not a current problem. Although actual Amy was a problem of a different nature.

"So, hey," Amy said. "I realized I had failed to share some things. I would like to do that now, although I realize this is kind of your place of business. Showing up at your place seemed stalkery and I didn't know for sure when you'd be home."

Dan glanced around but everyone was focused on packing up, or walking leisurely with their goodies. And if she was at his place, well he might either forgive her immediately or yell at her, so this was better. "Go ahead," he said bracing himself. He would let her talk, and then she could go home and feel better, and he could go home and try not to feel worse.

"So, I know I told you I had a lot of siblings. I maybe didn't explain that growing up, my mom, it wasn't that she didn't remember my birthday, it just wasn't a big deal to her. I never had a birthday party, none of my siblings did.

"And then when I was with Ryder, he remembered, but as far as whether he would be in town or not, was kind of - nope." Amy shook her head. "Not the point. Anyway, when Ryder showed up, I thought that was Ryder being Ryder. I hadn't realized the timing.

"I wasn't hiding it, I was planning to mention it when everyone arrived. I wasn't mad that you didn't show up on my birthday. I'm used to it. I'm used to people making dinner plans with me and not showing up. I can't count the number of times that's happened to me. And that was the thing, I don't want to be used to that. And yeah, now I know it was like an extreme case of coincidences, and I overreacted. So basically, I'm saying, I'm sorry I hurt you. I know you didn't mean to hurt me."

She looked at the table he hadn't folded up, had only stripped the cloth from. "Can I put this down?"

Dan nodded. He was still processing everything she had said. He hadn't thought his family made a particularly big deal about birthdays. But he had had a party every year as a kid, even the years his mother was super sick. His dad still called him every year at the time he was born, 2:02 pm.

So yes, Amy had overreacted to him not showing up once. But maybe he had reacted based on his own experience and not factored in hers.

Amy pulled a container out of the reusable shopping bag she had rested on the table. "So, I tried to look up if there was such a thing as birthday soup, and there is but it is seaweed. We haven't discussed seaweed so that seemed like an apology gift that might not be received in the manner it was intended."

"There's a birthday soup? Fascinating." Dan had not heard of birthday soup. He waved for her to continue. He wanted Amy finish talking so that she could go away and stop piercing his heart with those brown eyes of hers.

"Yes. So, I went with cake." She popped open the box and inside was a small rectangular cake with what looked like chocolate icing. "Oh, also, I should tell you I was afraid you were going to hurt me because I'm falling in love with you. And you could. Hurt me that is. But I didn't mean to hurt you also. Or more. So, okay, that's everything."

He nodded. He understood wanting to protect yourself from hurt. One of the things with being a small business owner was you had to take a ton of leaps of faith. It wasn't for everyone. He was used to going with his gut, and hoping everything worked out, even as he made backup plans for if it didn't. But maybe he'd been too willing to cut his losses on Amy.

"Okay, bye," she said.

"Amy, wait." She paused and his heart rate slowed to halfway normal. If he trusted this folding table, he would have leapt over it to make sure she didn't leave. Or, to make sure she at least heard him before he left.

"I'm sorry too. It was a string of coincidences, but I should have figured out a way to keep you from worrying. And yeah, I was hurt when I found out it was your birthday. I assumed it was a big deal and I was being penalized for not making an event I didn't have all the info on. But I'm falling in love with you too. Actually, I'm already in love with you. I can wait for you to catch up."

"Oh," Amy said. The smile moved over her face and Dan found he wasn't out of smiles after all. He smiled and he kissed her. Then he let Mateo take the stuff back to the kitchen.

Chapter 22

Amy: Hey, Ryder. Dan and I have something to tell you.

    Dan was added to the chat

Dan: Hey, Ryder. Amy and I wanted to let you know we're dating.

Amy: And in love.

Dan: I'm not sure he needs that much detail.

Amy: I just wanted to be clear.

Ryder: Oh, hey, sorry folks, I was on an airplane. But wow, great news. So does this mean I'm never getting Amy to move back to Pennsylvania or now I have a better chance of getting Dan to Pennsylvania?

Dan: I am not moving to Pennsylvania, Ryder.

Ryder: It would be just as close to your dad. And it has my parents and me.

Dan: Dude, you are like never home.

Amy: Someone had to say it.

Ryder: I have news for you two too. I accepted a new job with the Traveling Kitchen.

Dan: That's awesome.

Amy: Cool!

Ryder: So part of what I'm looking for is chefs who like to travel.

Dan: uerherhwehr

Dan: Sorry, Amy pinched me. So yeah, no dude. Can't leave the soup business unattended. Or apparently Amy.

Amy: Hey Ryder, that sounds like a lot of fun. And at least you'll be assured of great food when you travel. Send us lots of pics.

Ryder: Okay, talk to ya'll later. And congrats.

Amy and Dan put their phones down on her coffee table.

"So like no travel, ever? Is that the rule?" Dan asked.

"God no," Amy said. "But do you want to be a traveling chef?"

"No. But feeding people in crisis has some appeal."

"I'm sure we can think of other ways to do that. And I'm not saying you can't take a job with lots of travel. This new funding line, might have me doing travel. We just have to figure things out."

"With cake?"

"There could be cake. But is cake what you really want right now?" Amy asked.

Dan looked carefully at her. "Um no." He leaned and kissed her. Food was not a concern for quite some time.

The End

Acknowledgements

First, thanks again to Jackie Barbosa, who sparked the idea that led to this story. I have two other stories, including *Repeated Burn* that came about because of her suggesting a theme, and clearly the bouncy balls of ideas that my brain can sometime be appreciates someone who grabs one of the balls and says that one.

Also thanks to Carrie Lomax who generously reviewed an earlier version of this story.

I always thank my all my English teachers, and this past year the wonderful Sally Alexander passed away, Sally was wonderful and providing constructive feedback in ways that made you certain that she wanted the story to be yours but better and that she believed you could do it. It was wonderful to have that delightful combo so early. (And Ms. Rogers, Ms. Caterini, Ms. Wheat, and Ms. Case also did that. I have been so lucky.)

This story was initially released on Ream[1] in serial format, so thanks to all the folks who supported that.

Also reviews are always so important, please consider leaving one on your site of choice.

Newsletter for info on new releases and what I'm reading and writing can be found here: https://buttondown.email/talkapedia

ARC team signup is here: https://forms.gle/rXz2iqt6VaR8aq6F7

---

1. https://reamstories.com/tarakennedy

Also By Tara Kennedy

Bait Girl – A Young Adult Short Story
City Complications Series – Adult Contemporary Romance:
Aloha to You –Novella
Undercover Bridesmaid –Novel
Hot Bartender –Novel
City Entanglements Series: Adult Contemporary Romance:
Repeated Burn – Novella
Bored by the Billionaire – Novella
Clear as Ice – Novella
Not an Ending – a bonus epilogue available to newsletter subscribers
Of Kings and Queens - Novella
Too Busy Romance series: Adult Contemporary Romance
Troubled by Love – Novella
The 6 Times We Slept Together Just Once – Coming Fall 2023!
Non-Fiction:
Let's Talk About Fictional Sex
Find info on where to buy them at www.tarakennedy.com/books[1]

---

1. http://www.tarakennedy.com/books

About the Author

Tara Kennedy was born and raised in Washington, DC. By day she wrangles bureaucracy and by night she writes tales of folks smooching and trying to forge their way in this world. Tara also knits, reads, watches TV, and drinks lots and lots of tea. She is trying to break a Twitter habit.

You can find more at www.tarakennedy.com

Repeated Burn

Chapter 1

Raven's first sign that this day wasn't going to go as planned was when her metro card wouldn't swipe on the bus. She swiped it again and still got the horrifying buzz of no money. She smiled at the bus driver and glanced nervously back at the dude pressed up behind her as she fumbled for her wallet, counting out quarters to drop into the slot. By then the last remaining seats on the early morning bus were taken.

Raven was on her feet most of the day, the life of a bakery/coffee shop owner never involved as much sitting and eating cake as others thought. The forty minutes on the bus in the morning was the quietest part of the day. The ride back in the afternoon from her shop in DC over the Maryland line to where she could afford to live to the part of DC got a little rowdier.

Raven sent herself an email reminder to check on her metro card. It auto-debited from her account, but metro probably changed something. She'd have to remember to log in and fix it. Preferably before she forgot and got on the metro to get to the women's small business meetup that she ran tonight.

Raven entered the Purple Hazelnut through the back, turning only the lights in the kitchen on as she moved through checking and setting things up. They opened up at 6:30. Any earlier signs of life had the coffee hounds pounding on the door. She loved the coffee hounds, each and every one of their blessedly caffeine addicted souls, but she was not ready to face them before opening time. She usually got through the whole bus routine without having to actually talk to anyone.

Raven heard a thunk and glanced out at the glass front of the shop, wondering if Mr. Henry was back. He'd been staying in a shelter, but had told her a few days ago he had a line on some short term housing.

She didn't see anyone outside. The register beeped at her for keeping the drawer open, so she popped it shut. Raven looked back at the glass. The small thing she had thought was a shadow from the tree on the sidewalk was a bundle of clothes. Or a person. The first coffee urn beeped. Raven poured two coffees and sipped part of the first one. Not Mr. Henry. The dark ponytail was too long, and Mr. Henry definitely did not get professional highlights.

Raven unlocked the front door and leaned out. "We're not open just yet, but can I offer you some coffee?"

The head popped up and Raven realized what her brain had been trying to tell her. Those were the signature highlights of one Sienna George. She kept the hand with the coffee out. A small tiny part of her wanted to dump it on Sienna's perfect hair.

Sienna wasn't just a pretty young thing who managed to garner a minor amount of social media fame two years ago as the girl who didn't know her top was see through. No, Sienna was also the woman Raven's ex Russel had cheated on her with. Raven had later, people were always so happy to tell you later, discovered Russel had a habit of dating girls fresh out of college. He liked young women with great ideas, that he used, and supported, while taking large parts of the credit. And then as they began to garner success, or as they got to close to twenty-five, whichever came first, he selected a new one, and got that relationship going before he remembered to terminate the other. "Hi, Sienna. You want to come inside?"

Raven once tried to find Sienna to warn her about Russel. She followed Sienna to a club downtown before realizing there was no way for an ex to provide a useful warning. So she had left. But she and

Sienna had met before. Russel brought Sienna to Purple Hazelnut, just after Raven signed the lease. He told Raven they should hire Sienna for an advertising shoot. Raven had thanked her stars a few times that she hadn't had the money for that kind of advertising at the time. She would have been stuck with ads of her ex's new girlfriend on her shop materials, as if there weren't ghosts of fucking Russel all over this shop.

Sienna stood, and managed to look artfully sad and disheveled, which was impressive. Raven heard noises in the back. "Hang on, let me check with the baker." Sienna nodded and sat at the table just inside the door.

Having notified her employee, she moved back front, giving in and taking the chair across from Sienna. The smell of coffee brewing in the other two urns scented the air. They had twenty more minutes before they opened. She foolishly hoped that maybe Sienna could be on her way by then. Sienna looking artfully sad might distract the customers from their caffeine and their breakfast pastries.

"So, Sienna, what's happening?"

"He left me," Sienna whispered.

"I'm sorry," Raven said.

"He's been seeing her, for like three months. He even introduced her to me. Her name's Sage or some sort of spice."

Raven nodded. Another part of the Russel pattern. She had found out later, Elsie, the woman who Russel dated before Raven had been on a trip to Europe when Russel and Raven first met. Russel had told Raven he'd just gotten out of a relationship. It turned out he considered being in different continents a separation. He hadn't let Elsie know he'd moved on until she got back to a half empty apartment.

Raven heard the timers go off on the ovens in the kitchen. "Well, Sienna, I'm sorry to hear that. I need to finish getting ready to open, but I can bring you a pastry or something."

"That bastard is on a beach with both our money," Sienna muttered.

Raven pulled out her phone and brought up her personal banking app. Well, shit. Metro hadn't screwed up. Because her bank account was empty.

MARCUS GEORGE LIKED having friends who were bartenders. But sometimes they kept you out late trying the new cocktail menu they were debuting the next day. The hotel industry didn't ever sleep. These days Marcus worked in the back office side of things at the Union Camden, where they worked something closer to office hours. Rolling in just before ten he waved at the front desk staff. He walked straight to the fancy coffee machine.

"Late night," Rhian said leaning against the counter. Her dark hair was pinned up, and her skirt suit was crisp. She looked well-rested and fully functional.

He smiled. "Gotta keep those partying skills sharp, otherwise they atrophy."

"You would know," Rhian said.

"My buddy Xavier's got a new cocktail menu. You would like it," Marcus said.

"My liver wouldn't." Rhian said. "Besides, I like to save my pennies for shoes and purses."

"If you are paying for your own drinks you are doing it wrong," Marcus said.

"We can't all make friends everywhere we go. Finish making coffee and or let me get mine, party boy."

"Yes, ma'am." Marcus saluted and got the machine programmed and pressed start.

Back at his office, he went through the reports from shift leaders. He oversaw hospitality for more than the Union Camden location. Having started his career as a front desk team member, he found working where he saw front desk staff, lunched with housekeepers, it worked better than being at the hotel's corporate headquarters in Rockville. Plus the food and post work day nightlife was much better here in downtown DC.

His stomach growled and he figured it was lunchtime. His cell buzzed followed by a knock on his office door. Kyran, one of the concierge's, stood on the other side of the glass door.

"Hey, Kyran, everything okay?" he asked.

"You have visitors. Your sister and someone else."

"Ah, okay. You can bring them back." Marcus's sister Sienna didn't show up at the hotel much. Usually only when she had run out of money. There had been less of that since she started dating Russel with one l. He hoped that wasn't the person with his sister. But no, Kyran reappeared with Sienna in what he called her sad Sienna outfit, designer hoodie, and branded running tights, with chunky heels. Her friend was dressed cargo pants and a loose fitting top, paired with sneakers. He swore Sienna had once declared she couldn't be seen in public with people wearing sneakers, so maybe this was a sign his sister was maturing.

"She yours?" Sneakers girl asked.

"My sister?" He gestured to Sienna, who leaned forward and hugged him.

"Yeah. Cool." She reached out and patted the back of Sienna's shoulder. "You'll be fine, kid. See ya later." She turned around and walked back out. Marcus wanted her to come back and at least give him the scoop on why his sister was now sniffling in his shoulder. Sienna would tell him of course. With their Mom having retired back to Hawaii it was just them two left of their family on the East coast. He was going to let Sienna cry and borrow money.

"Sienna, do you need water or soda or something?" He couldn't remember if she was still doing the sugar cleanse.

She mumbled something he couldn't quite make words. He tried again. "Water?"

Sienna lifted her head up. "Do you have sparkling?"

"Sure. Why don't you sit." He guided her to the guest chair. He grabbed the sparkling water in two different flavors from the kitchen area.

He held out both to Sienna. She took the lemon, and he popped the raspberry for himself leaning against the edge of his desk.

"He left me." Sienna sniffled. "For someone else. Can you believe it?"

Marcus was certain that was a rhetorical question, so he adopted a sympathetic listening face.

"He was supposed to get me a gig doing the ad campaign for Sacred Cow Yoga and instead he left me for her."

"I'm sorry." Marcus was pretty sure Sienna meant the owner of Sacred Cow Yoga, not an actual Sacred Cow, but the details weren't important. Russel with one l promised Sienna he'd help her get a number of ad campaigns and Marcus had yet to see any of it come through. "Have you eaten lunch?"

Sienna shook her head.

"Let's go grab something across the street." He usually grabbed something from the hotel employee cafeteria. Sad Sienna could be distracting though, so away from his coworkers might be better. "Come on." He waved at Rhian on his way out, hanging on to Sienna's elbow as he guided her back outside.

Once they were seated and had food ordered he got down to business. "Is your apartment okay?" he asked.

The new batch of tears bubbling up in Sienna's eyes told him his worst fears were right on target. So yeah, instead of a weekend of fun ahead, he was going to have a weekend of sister wrangling. This definitely called for more coffee.

More of Repeated Burn *is available at various etailers and in print. More info here:* www.tarakennedy.com/books[1]

---

1. http://www.tarakennedy.com/books